Uncovered

L.M. Mountford

The Lord of Lust Publications

The Lord of Lust Publications

Published by The Lord of Lust Publications

ISBN: 978-1-83502-038-8

The story, all names, characters, and incidents portrayed in this production are fictitious. No identification with actual persons (living or deceased), places, buildings, and products is intended or should be inferred.

Book Cover by C. Lorraine Creatives

Edited by Readabit Editing

3rd edition 2025

The Lord of Lust Publications
Indie Publishing for Indie Authors

UNCOVERED

The Lord of Lust
L.M. Mountford
Award winning Author

One

 The shower stall was thick with steam, the hum of the motor reverberating through the walls as fat beads of condensation ran down the natural brown stone tiles and fogged glass door. Tipping her head back into the spray and sweeping the sodden, honey-coloured tresses from her eyes, Mina Carring uttered a low, throaty moan as the scalding water pelted her naked body, washing the stresses of the day away.

She longed for moments like these. After a long day posing for cameras and listening to photographers and directors screaming at each other like toddlers contesting for their favourite toy, there was nothing more relaxing than a scald-ing-hot shower.

And it really hadn't been her day.

Even from the outset, nothing had seemed to go to plan. It all started with her sleeping through her alarm and over-sleeping by more than half an hour. Then the coffee maker had died mid-brew, forcing her to start the day without her vital morning fix. Later, matters were only made worse by the combination of morning rush hour and a minor accident that had left her stranded in a long, snaking queue of traffic down Route 405, more than an hour after she was supposed to meet with her agent for a late breakfast. Finally, there was that debacle of a photo-shoot.

While few, *knowledgeable* individuals would describe the life of a model and actress as easy, that one shoot had just about taken the biscuit. It should have been so simple, so easy. Just one shoot, little more than a day's work, modelling a new fashion line for a new European branded clothing store that would be opening on Montana Avenue sometime in the summer.

There had just been one problem. The French photog-rapher commissioned for the shoot considered himself a born-again Guy Bourdin, but seemed only to bear a striking resemblance to a toad, and had insisted on having the natural lighting and mood of every shot to be exact to his vision. Yet there were not enough hours in the day or positions of the sun, and in the end, an afternoon's shoot had to be spread over three days. Today had been the last and was an easy two hours posing on a rock rising out of the surf and walking across the deserted stretch of beach. However, it

seemed Pierre the Toad had woken up on the wrong side
of his fishpond and before she had even had a chance to
change, he was screaming that 'this was wrong' or 'that
was out of place'.

In the end, chewing her bottom lip was all she could do
to stop herself from telling him just where he could stick
his precious vision.

Despite the heat of the shower, Mina shuddered at the
memory. She'd so desperately wanted to leave, to quit and
go on with her day the way she'd been planning to for
some weeks. She wanted to go out to Griffith Observatory
with Mark and their parents for lunch before taking them
on an expensive shopping trip down La Brea Avenue.
After all, it wasn't every day her little stepbrother turned
21. Yet the restrictions in her contract forced her to
finish the job, regardless of her prior engagements or that
slimy, self-aggrandising toad's attitude problems.

Now it was up to her to make it up to Mark.

Reluctantly, she hit the button to shut off the water
before throwing open the glass door. Wet and dripping,
but feeling fully refreshed, she let the little rivulets of
water run off her before stepping out from beneath the
dripping shower head and onto the fluffy white bath
mat that encircled the stall. Courtesy of the shower, her
spacious ensuite was warm and misty, but a single open
window hinted at the tiniest chill. Her skin prickled at the
delicious contrast as she took a towel off the heated rail
and patted herself down. Vigorously towelling her hair
with one hand, she opened the door to her connecting
master bedroom and sauntered inside.

Spacious and airy, she'd had its walls painted a passionate shade of crimson shortly after purchasing the property and furnished it with fittings of deep oak, making the room feel more intimate. Shafts of deep red light filtered through the gaps in the drawn curtains to flood the room with a natural illumination as the sun sank beneath the distant horizon. However, it was the south-facing windows and outer balcony, offering splendid views overlooking Beverly Hills, that made this her favourite room in the house.

She had already selected her clothes for tonight from the walk-in-wardrobe and had neatly laid them out across the queen-size bed's black Egyptian cotton sheets. Forgoing underwear, she dropped the towel unceremoniously onto the floor and tugged her black slim jeans up her long, willowy legs and over her buttocks. She deftly fastened the buttons, then pulled a powder-blue, long-sleeved, babydoll-style top over her head. Though not tight or revealing, the thin fabric moulded to her still damp skin to leave nothing to the imagination. It made her feel naughty, and the thought of Mark seeing her like this ignited a warm tingling feeling in the pit of her stomach.

No! Stop it. That's not why you're going to see him.

When fully dressed, she crossed the bedroom in several quick strides to her dressing table, where arrayed around the oval vanity mirror, was a variety of jewellery boxes, perfumes, brushes, creams and other beauty utensils. Her likeness glowered back from within the glass.

Mina tried to picture the person who had been looking back at her five years before, and then the little nine year-old girl she'd been fifteen years ago. So much had changed. She felt older, drawn, and tired with the weight of a lifetime's mistakes forever bearing down on her.

Yet still so much was the same.

The same wavy golden hair, angular features, and sparkling azure eyes that had won her that first audition peered back at her. She had been a meek, quiet child back then and her father had thought the experience might help her come out of her shell. He'd had to drag her to that audition kicking and screaming, after a director saw her perform the role of the Pied Piper in her school play and suggested she audition for a role in his new movie, *Eternity's Wisps*. The film had been a low-budget B-movie, a science-fiction collage of *Star Wars* and *Star Trek* with just the smouldering, gritty hint of *Sin City* thrown in. It was the ill-born brainchild of a writer long past his best trying to rekindle the forgotten glory of the '80s space-race movies, and had held all the prospects for success as a thriller starring Robert Pattinson.

Considering her reflection, she took a shiny black comb inlaid with lapis in hand and began brushing the tangles from her hair until it framed her face and fell down past her shoulders in a wash of sun-kissed curls.

Had her mother looked like her when she was her age?

Mina often pondered the question, even though she knew she would never have the answer. She had not known her mother. She had been too young to remember when she had vanished into the night without a word. Her father never spoke of her, no matter how much she had pestered him. Out of respect for him, Mina had never searched for her, never hired a private investigator or reached out in any way, despite numerous offers from several prime time talk shows.

There were no photos of her in the house, no traces or details online. It was almost as if she'd vanished off the face of the earth and all Mina had left was a name.

Angela Willis.

The name brought her no comfort or rush of recognition however, but installed only the deepest sense of sadness that threatened to overwhelm her in a surge of suppressed emotion whenever she thought of it. She had questions, so many questions. Was her mother alive? Where was she? Why did she do it? Did Mina mean so little to her? Was it something she'd done? The list went on and on. She had forgotten how many times she'd asked herself those poignant questions and bore that inevitable, terrible weight of doubt and self-loathing. Yet, as much as she longed to know the truth, Mina had never wanted to hear the answers. Some things were better left unknown. And as much as people claimed it would set you free, the truth could be a far more bitter pill to swallow than ignorance.

Utterly engrossed in her thoughts and her grooming, she didn't notice the figure coming up behind her, just out of sight of the mirror, and almost jumped out of her skin in fright when a pair of strong arms suddenly coiled around her waist and drew her backward. Without thinking, she made to lash out with the comb and break free of her captor, but then went limp, the makeshift shiv slipping from nerveless fingers as thin lips teased the sensitive place on the back of her neck, just behind her left ear. Her knees went weak and a low moan escaped her.

Only two men knew about that little spot.

"You look beautiful tonight," Jason whispered against her throat, sending delicious shivers down her spine as his fingers slipped beneath the waistline of her top to glide across her flat stomach. A tingling sensation zipped down to her centre. Damn him, how did he always know just how to touch her?

"Mmm...thanks, but I really need to go-oh...I'm already running late and Mark's party is-oh, god..." Words failed her as he began laying fiery little nips and kisses along the curve of her neck before ravenously gnawing on the sensitised tendons. She noted that he hadn't shaved today and her toes curled at the feeling of his stubble-roughened chin as it brushed against her softer skin.

Jason William Scott Stoker had been her boyfriend for the better part of three years. They'd met while filming *The Devil's Messenger*. He had been her co-star and character's love interest, and they had instantly hit it off, their chemistry as sizzling off-screen as it was on. Though she couldn't explain it, there was just something about his geeky sense of humour and Newcastle accent that she found enthralling. Seized by the passion of the moment, she swivelled in his arms to catch his lips in a hungry kiss while she tangled her fingers in his dark mop of frizzy hair.

The embrace was instantly hot and heavy. Taking the offensive, Mina eagerly curled a long leg around his thigh while she traced her tongue across his lips, demanding entry. Groaning a low sound, he acquiesced, his hands moving down the curve of her spine to paw her derrière through the tight denim. Though tall and lanky, he was uncommonly strong and she couldn't help but utter her own low moan as he drew her closer, allowing her to feel the weight of his desire pressing against her, stoking the fire that suddenly burned inside her. Then their tongues met in a fierce dance, their teeth gnashing violently as they battled for dominance, manoeuvring blindly back towards the bed.

Almost knocking her heel on the bed's heavy oaken frame, she trailed her fingers down his neck to press against his upper torso before she pivoted, breaking the embrace to send him tumbling to the bed. He had a handsome face, rugged with a defined jaw, an easy smile, and emerald-green eyes that could make her go weak in the knees with just one look.

Smirking at his stupefied expression, she bent over his prone figure, her hair spilling over her shoulders to glide lightly over his cheeks, and kissed him again, but it was only a chaste, teasing touch, a ghost of her former passion, and she drew back before it could develop into something more. Confused, Jason's eyes narrowed and he shot her an incredulous look as she rose to her feet, but she met the stare with only an apologetic smile.

"Sorry, tiger, but I'm already late." She pivoted on her heel and went back to the dresser. The mauled reflection that greeted her had her lips pressed together in a tight line. Nearly tutting in disgust at the sight of the red blotches on her neck and swollen lips, Mina shook out the dishevelled, and quite unrepairable ruin of her hair before tussling it with her fingers, trying to bring some order to the chaos.

"Do you want me to come with you?"

Her eyes darted to his reflection in the mirror. He was now propped up on the bed by his elbows, his eyes bright as he watched her with an almost lazy smile.

"No, its fine." Casting a look across the cabinet, she selected one of her foundations and began applying it to the red marks. "This will just be a quick visit. Dad and Alexis are having dinner at Le Cœur de la Merso Mark is having some friends from university round. I'll just drop his gifts off, say sorry for missing him earlier and wish him a happy birthday. Then I'll be on my way home."

Jason's eyebrow quirked at her. "All that, just for a quick visit?"

Men!

Placing the cosmetic back on the dresser with a roll of her eyes, she then selected her favourite lipstick from the selection. "A girl has to look her best."

"You're always at your best. If only you'd let yourself see it."

There was a depth of emotion in his voice Mina rarely heard there. It made her feel uneasy, as though the heavy knot in her gut was rising to block her throat. Her fingers trembled as she applied the lipstick and she tried to swallow, to force it down.

Don't say it-

"I love you."

She stilled, his words striking her like the crack of a bullwhip. Ice ran through her veins as their eyes met in the mirror and she saw the desperate pleading within them.

Please, not again.

At the end of her silent appeal, her mind ran to the two small, velvet-lined boxes he hid in the bottom draw of his bedside table beneath his socks. She knew he'd kept them. Had he bought another? God, she hoped not, since the thought of rejecting him again weighed like a stone in her heart. Why couldn't he understand she wasn't that kind of woman?

Jason frowned at her silence, then pushed away from the bed to sit straight-backed with a resigned sigh. "Can't you say it. Just once?"

I wish I could

But she wouldn't lie to him. Forcibly swallowing the lump in her throat, Mina closed the lipstick and placed it back amongst the others before wheeling around and giving him her best reassuring smile. It did not quite reach her eyes however. Almost cool, they held his imploring look as she walked towards the bed, her feet seeming to glide over the soft carpet without a sound. Then, she bent forward and rested both hands on the footboard, until his eyes were level with her breasts. She drew in a breath, just enough to lift the swells of her bosom and emphasize the way the very thin fabric stretched over her cleavage.

She wanted to love him, she really did. He was a good man, fun and dependable and deserving of someone much better than her. But her heart was a fickle bitch, devoting itself to a lover, opting to never truly open up. She'd seen where that road led and what came of giving herself to someone completely.

Despite himself, Jason's eyes flickered downward at the movement and lingered there, the shape of his manhood rising sharp and strong against his jeans, tenting the otherwise slack denim. Mina smirked, her plush tongue darting out suggestively over her rosy lips. "Hold that thought for me, lover boy." Jason's eyes darted back up, but she was already backing away. "Wait up for me and I promise, when I get home, we can pick up where we left off."

She felt cold steel against her fingertips as her hand blindly closed around the door handle. "Until then, here's a little preview..." As her left hand pulled the door open, her right grabbed the hem of her top and dragged it up, flashing him a provocative view of her cleavage.

Then she was gone.

Her heart thundered with excitement as she bolted before the door had even closed behind her, a broad smile on her lips as she envisioned Jason chasing her through the house before having his way with her against the door. Pushing her top back into place, she almost ran down the house's spiralling staircase into the airy foyer. Slipping on a designer pair of brown leather boots and the matching jacket, she grabbed her keys off the oak side table and the plastic shopping bag beside it containing Mark's presents, before opening the ebony front door and stepping out into the cool evening air.

The sky was a dwindling tapestry of pink and orange beneath a sinking sea of violet, the sun long hidden behind the western horizon. Los Angeles was nothing but a ghostly silhouette, the city a prisoner in the twilight purgatory that divided night from day.

Bathed in the golden glow of the hanging iron lamp, she walked past the four huge columns of pale alabaster stone that supported the upper balcony, and down the porch's three wide steps. In her wake, the heavy door slid shut with a booming bang.

Parked in the centre of the ringed pebble and coral driveway, and polished to a high shine, was her sleek, black, Luxury Ride Lexus RX 350. Clicking the key to unlock the vehicle before pocketing the fob, she clambered into the driver's seat, carefully placing the shopping bag in the passenger seat's foot-space. She dragged the door shut behind her, strapped on her seat belt, took off the handbrake, and pressed the ignition. The engine bellowed to life, emitting a deep rumble that had the seat vibrating deliciously beneath her. Mina slipped the shifter into drive and put her foot to the accelerator, sending the SUZ roaring forward. Pressed back into her seat by the sudden motion, she drove around the doughnut-shaped driveway, passed through the high-arched, black iron gate that marked the end of her 1.2 acre estate as it swung open automatically at her approach, and without looking, turned sharply onto the winding street beyond.

Two

 Turning off at the lights, leaving Benedict Canyon Drive and the majority of the traffic in her rear-view mirror, she sped down the long Sherman Oaks Boulevard. The road teemed with clusters of convenience stores and a dozen or so minor residential streets, each lined with modest two-storey homes that branched off on either side. Counting each junction off, she swerved down the eighth to find the street chock-a-block with parked cars. Though her father's house was more than halfway down the stretch, the sheer number of cars parked along it forced her to pull over beside the dark silhouette of

a broken streetlight standing on the curve of the cul-de-sac that ended the road.

Overhead, the sky was black, night's cloak having fully descended. There was no moon, but stars twinkled merrily overhead, dotted here and there, shining brightly against the all-consuming blackness in their ageless tapestries across the celestial sphere.

Turning off the ignition, she undid her seat belt, opened the door, and clambered out into the night, a shiver running down her spine as her hair began to flutter in the wind. Despite it being mid-October, there was an unseasonable bite in the night air and she drew her jacket close before retrieving Mark's presents from the passenger side. Reaching into her jacket pocket and locking the SUV with a click of the fob, Mina started down the left-hand sidewalk, past nine near-identical, modest yet homely properties, and up the paved driveway.

Even from the bottom of the street, her father's house was easy to spot. Parked across the sloping garden were half a dozen cars and a colourful banner draped from the roof, proclaiming 'Happy Birthday Mark' in red and gold glitter, but only half visible amidst the low glow of nearby street lights. Party music boomed from the open windows and door. As she walked up the drive, a group of young men were loitering on the doorstep, smoking and conversing amongst themselves in hushed tones.

Spotting her approach, the one that stood farthest back, leaning against the doorframe beneath the porch light with a cigarette dangling from his lips, gave a slight nod. The excessive amount of gel in his flaming red hair caused it to glisten like amber at the movement. All at once, the group fell silent and wheeled about to confront her. By their sheepish expressions, she could tell they were up to no good but she chose not to say anything. When they realised she was not a cop, the group begrudgingly shifted a step to let her pass.

Curls of pale smoke weaved around her as she stepped onto the porch, and the air was heavy with a sickly sweet aroma that had her stomach churning with the first breath.

Marijuana!

Taking care not to look any of them in the eye, Mina carried on without a second's pause. She could feel the heat of their lecherous leers on her as she passed, following her every step and giving her an all-encompassing once-over before finally settling upon her backside. They watched her with all the subtlety of a pack of starving hyenas studying a zebra herd, sending a shiver that had nothing to do with the cold crawling up her spine.

Just as she was about to cross the house's threshold, one of them muttered something she couldn't hear that had the rest sniggering. Pausing mid-stride, Mina had a momentary impulse to wheel about and ask them if they'd like to take a picture, but then she put it from her mind. They weren't worth the breath.

Inside, she found a scene straight out of *American Pie*. Music was blaring from an iPod boom dock speaker system that had been set up on the living room coffee table. Across the narrow foyer, she could see an aluminium beer keg in the kitchen amidst a buffet-style bonanza of party foods on disposable plates. And there were people everywhere either commingling in gangs of three or five, or gyrating mindlessly against one another to whatever musical abomination happened to be playing over the hi-fi.

The only thing missing is Seann William Scott shouting profanity.

As she surveyed the scene, Mina could hardly contain her look of amazement. While she'd known Mark had been given run of the house for the party, their parents having gone out for dinner and a show before spending the night in a hotel, she'd certainly never expected something so very, well, un-Mark.

She just hoped they didn't destroy the house. It had not been easy getting her father to agree to the idea...

She should have known better than to let the conversation turn to the matter of money, let alone direct it there. But when they had drifted to the inevitable topic of Mark's 21st birthday in two weeks, he'd said her stepbrother would be home from university that weekend and had asked to have the house for a party. Mina was so excited she couldn't help herself. Mark had never been very social. While his friends had been playing in the park and going round each other's houses after school, he'd spent hours playing Diablo and Crash Bandicoot.

In all the years they'd lived together, he'd never had more than a handful of friends round so there was no danger of the party getting out of hand, however her father had still been reluctant. She, on the other hand, made no effort to hide her enthusiasm. Without thinking, she'd offered to make arrangements for him and her stepmother to have dinner at her favourite seafood restaurant and then spend the night in a top hotel on La Cienega Boulevard.

"No, Mina."

"But Daddy."

"Absolutely not," he snapped, his voice dangerously level as he watched her from behind the rim of his tea cup. His deep green eyes that had beamed at the sight of her only an hour before, were suddenly cold and impassive, an unmovable expression she knew all too well. "I've told you before, I pay my own way."

Mina just wanted to squint, leer, and stick her tongue out. For a moment she considered telling him his way couldn't cover so much as a starter at Le Cœur de la Mer, but then thought better of it.

As Sid James said, 'We're not called John Bull for nothing.'

They were in the Denny's on Tiverton Avenue, seated at their usual booth in the far corner opposite the row of windows looking out at the tinted windows and clay brown bricks of the Palomino Restaurant and Bar across the road, having their usual brunch. It was unusually quiet for ten o'clock on a Sunday morning, with only a few groups of two and three at a handful of tables and one young blond waitress serving the floor. There were times Mina would have been glad of the solitude. She missed spending quality time with her father, sitting back on the sofa and discussing their day while watching his old *Only Fools and Horses* videos like they had when she was little. At this moment, she would have been glad of the distraction, or any distraction for that matter.

"Hiya, is everything okay? Can I get you anything else?" the waitress asked, pausing at their table with a tray of dirties in each hand, her notepad tucked in her uniform trousers' back pocket. Barely more than sixteen, with a head of fire-kissed curls hastily dragged back into a bun and an uneasy but friendly smile, she paid Mina little notice and the actress could have kissed her for her timing.

"No. We're fine, thank you," James Carring said, his eyes softening as he lowered the cup to the table and smiled amiably at the girl. "Could we have our cheque please?"

"Certainly, sir, I'll be right ba..." The words died on her lips as she turned to carry on to the door leading through to the kitchen and her eyes fell on the older blonde. Sparkling blue pools widened in recognition. "Oh, my God! You're Mina Car...well of course you are...I mean I just didn't...I'm such a fan an...I just loved...and um...well, could I, that is, if you don't mind, may I..." She seemed on the verge of a breakdown. In her excitement, her hands were shaking so violently it was a miracle both trays didn't go clattering to the floor. Then a sudden calm fell over her and she took a deep breath before asking "can I have your autograph?"

Mina felt her cheeks growing hot and she had the sudden impulse to bury her face behind one of the standing menus on the table, or look out the window at the Palomino to watch the slow train of people walking the sidewalk. Or anywhere but at the waitress watching her expectantly and who looked like she might burst into tears at any moment. However, also very much aware of the eyes suddenly swivelling in their direction, with more than a few threatening camera phones, Mina chose not to humiliate the teen further. Her lips curled in a reassuring smile. "Sure."

James Carring smiled bemusedly, his brow quirking with ill-disguised amusement, the way all parents did when they knew their children were embarrassed.

"Really!" the girl beamed, then her cheeks reddened and she looked away sheepishly. "Oh, my God. I'm so embarrassed, I can't believe I just said that, but thank you. Thank you. Let me just get your bill and I'll be right back." With that, the waitress whirled around in a pirouette worthy of the Bolshoi, all but ran past several diners signalling for service, and through to the kitchen without dropping so much as a spoon.

Mina watched the younger woman disappear behind the swinging door with her mouth open. Half expecting to see her come bustling back in at any moment, she turned back to find her father had already taken his wallet from his coat pocket and was fingering through several twenties. She was about to tell him she'd cover it as he had paid last time, but he seemed to know her mind and shot her an imperious look that held her tongue.

Easing back into the red padding of her seat with a defeated sigh, she turned her eyes down to her unfinished chicken salad. She prodded one of the apple slices with her fork, the flesh all but saturated with dressing. He never changed. Why did he always have to be so English? Not only did he always insist on paying, but he doggedly refused to accept her help, even when he knew he couldn't afford it.

"Well," she began after a moment, steeling herself for a second assault. "How about this? I know the maître d'. If you give him a ring and tell him you're my dad, he'll give you a discount."

James's finger paused and he looked up from the notes to fix his daughter with a sceptical eye. "A discount?"

"Yes, just a discount." She gave him her sweetest smile, apprehension winding her insides into a chain of tight knots under her father's scrutinising gaze. That very look had made her crumble often, made her feel like he was seeing through her masks to the little girl she'd once been.

For an instant, Mina thought her father might press her, to try and ferret out a lie. But he gave only a small nod, then drew forty dollars from his wallet and placed it down on the table. "Okay."

"Okay?"

He nodded again and Mina couldn't help the trace of a smile that curled at the corner of her lips as she dragged her handbag from where she'd pinned it between the table and her foot and began rummaging inside for her phone. It wasn't a complete lie. Grey if not white. She was on first-name terms with the maître d' and he would let him have a table for two at a knocked down price, but only because Mina would be calling later today to explain the situation and arrange to have the lion's share of the bill diverted to her account.

Her father watched her impassively as she copied the number from her phone onto a napkin. From his unmovable expression, it was hard to say whether or not he believed her, but he knew well enough his wife wanted Mark to enjoy his 21st and James Carring would do almost anything to see his wife smile. He took the napkin from her when she handed it across the table, glanced at it and then tucked it into his pocket along with the wallet.

"You're still very fond of the boy, aren't you?" he asked without looking at her.

Mina gave a small shrug. "He's my little brother." There was little point in denying it. Their parents had known how close she and Mark had become while growing up together. Though if they'd had any notion of how far that relationship had gone, she doubted they'd be quite so complacent. "What kind of sister would I be if I weren't?"

"Yes."

Across the diner, the waitress burst through the door to the kitchen, punched a few details into the computer at the pay station, and was then weaving a path back to their booth, bill in hand. James smiled at the look on the girl's face, the way she tried to appear professional but couldn't quite hide her excitement, then shot his daughter a sideways glance and added, "But he's only your stepbrother."

With her ears ringing from the raucous bombardment, Mina slipped into the mass of writhing hormones and weaved through the crowd. It had been several years since she last visited the house, but she found it had hardly changed and remained much the way she remembered it. The house had the same mocha carpet and pale beige walls adorned with hanging family photos. The same sturdy box-television sat in the living room, and cabinets sat opposite the grey four-seater settee, presently a makeshift bed for an amorous young couple engrossed in a heated game of tonsil-hockey. Her father's faded chocolate leather Barcalounger in the far corner, beside his antique and securely locked liquor cabinet, was forgotten and almost completely buried beneath a mound of coats. Yet there was no sign of her stepbrother.

Depositing the bag amongst the other gifts encircling the television, only half pleased to see it was by far the largest, she turned on her heel and decided to check the kitchen. Mina tried to ignore the heads twisting in her direction as she edged around the improvised dance floor, pressing a path through the revellers, eyes peeled for any glimpse of Mark.

Yet, as she weaved between the tight press of bodies, Mina couldn't help but curiously eye their peculiar array of body art, hairstyles, and tattered ill-fitting attire. Was this what the 'kids' were into these days? At only 24, was she already so old? Then again, were they really so strange? When she was in school, she could recall baggy clothes, raiding shopping centres armed with spray paint, losing her virginity in the back seat of a 1969 Dodge Charger, and even occasionally snorting coke in clubs. But the phases that had come and gone as quickly as David Beckham's haircuts. Was this merely how the modern youth rebelled against authority?

When she found Mark, would he still be that geeky, awkward teenager, or resemble the ill-fated love child of a central African tribesman and a '70s punk rocker...

She passed between the already ajar French doors to the large adjoining dining room, where a large group sat playing rounds of billiards, with their clothes as the stakes. Moving through to the kitchen, Mina muttered a curse under her breath.

Small but also practical, the kitchen had wide windows that looked out across the back garden, now swallowed in inky blackness. Fragments of light danced off the dull aluminium appliances, and the kitchen was as much a bustling hive of activity as it ever was. In the far corner, a tall, broad-shouldered man with rich black hair was talking to a beauty of a girl with a bob-cut of dirty-blond hair and whose high, bountiful bosom stretched the front of her tiny cotton sweater almost to ruin. By the windows, a trio of beer-splattered frat boys had made a game of juggling disposable cups and drinking a beer whenever they dropped one. There was a gaggle of girls gossiping and giggling, herds of boys posturing and showboating- yet still no sign of Mark.

A glint of gold caught her eye and a broad smile spread across her lips. Hung pride of place upon the inner wall in the sterling silver frame with swirling gold inlaid runes along the edges that she'd bought them for their last anniversary, was a photo from her father's wedding day. It showed him standing on Descanso Beach, with pale white sand underfoot and the Catalina Casino sitting just above the sea's calm blue waters in the background. He was resplendent in his tailored three-piece wedding suit and the top hat that hid his salt and pepper hair, and stood with a protective arm around his new bride, Alexis. She and Mark were there too. Mark, the nervous six-year-old best man, half hidden behind the groom's legs, she the beaming flower girl at the head of the party, clutching a bouquet of white roses and clad in a gorgeous ivory satin gown that was an almost exact miniature duplicate of the bride's wedding dress.

Had it really been fifteen years ago? It was almost inconceivable, yet the last decade had just seemed to fly by so fast. She had developed the habit of losing track of time. She could remember that day so vividly, however. Mark had been nervous, so nervous that when the moment came for him to pass the rings, his hand had been shaking so violently he had dropped them in the middle of the aisle. Alexis was the very definition of a blushing bride, graceful, demure, and utterly beyond all reproach even as she *blindly* tossed the bouquet in such a way that only Mina could have caught it. And her father...Mina had never seen him so happy. All throughout the day he had beamed with joy and just the sight of his new bride coming down the aisle had lifted years from his weathered face, banishing the spectre that had loomed over his shoulders for so many years.

The spectre was of course her mother. A ghost of a memory that had chased him from his home on the outskirts of the town of Bodmin, Cornwall, and hounded him across the Atlantic. For eight long years, Mina had watched her father flounder in a sea of depression, her young heart tortured by the clawing feeling of utter helplessness from knowing there was nothing she could do to help or, worse still, that she was the cause. He never said it. He loved her, adored her and lavished her with all the affection a father owes to his child. Yet she had seen it nonetheless. She had seen it in his eyes, in those pools of emerald green in the rare, unguarded moments when his walls came down and he did not see his daughter. When there was no love, emotion, or feeling in his gaze, only a question. Why? For she was the living reminder of the woman he had loved and lost, the shadow of the woman who had torn out his heart...

A deep rumble from her stomach shattered her contemplations. Suddenly very aware she hadn't had any dinner, Mina shot a curious glance towards the food spread across the kitchen's long rectangular island counter. It was the typical party selection- BBQ chicken wings, cocktail sausages, crisps, nachos and, around the large aluminium keg, a ring of pizza boxes that glistened with cheese and toppings. The sight enticed another complaining rumble from her stomach.

Unable to resist, Mina walked over and helped herself to a large slice of pepperoni pizza, her mouth watering with the first breath of its heady aroma. Taking a large bite, she moaned appreciatively as the forbidden morsel flooded her senses with flavours, and she turned around to find a raven-haired Adonis towering over her.

"Hey, you're Mina, right?" Though noticeably quieter in the kitchen than the living room, he still had to raise his voice to be heard over the roar of the music. "Mina Carring, Mark's stepsister?" At her perplexed nod of affirmation, he grinned, revealing two perfect rows of pearly whites. "Remember me?"

Taken aback, Mina took a reflexive step back before giving him a once over while chewing the delicious mouthful of bread, spiced meat, and melted cheese. While she couldn't place where they might have come across each other before, upon closer inspection, there was something familiar about him. It wasn't his face, though he was certainly comely, in a smouldering, clean-shaven, square-jawed, Hugh Jackman and Luke Evans sort of way. It was his eyes- she had seen them before. They were blue, flecked with spots of gold, and seemed to gleam with a mischievousness that she was sure had stolen a fair few hearts. Yes, she knew those eyes from somewhere. Over his shoulder, she glimpsed the blonde standing with her arms crossed, looking very put out and glaring at Mina with undisguised hostility.

A name formed on the tip of her tongue, just out of reach...

His grin never faltered. "It's Daniel. Daniel Cornwell. You used to babysit me and Mark every Saturday."

His words struck her like a lightning bolt and Mina had to resist the impulse to spit her mouthful of pizza across the floor. Forcibly, she swallowed the mouthful.

"What! No, you can't be. Not little Danny." She was almost certain her jaw must have dropped and her eyes glanced towards one of Mark's old school year photos that hung on the kitchen wall, studying the dark-haired sprite standing next to Mark who had tormented her mercilessly every weekend. He may have grown taller, but there was no mistaking that impish grin. "Jesus Christ, you grew up."

Daniel's eyes twinkled mischievously. "Yeah... well, I haven't needed a babysitter for quite a while now."

"So I see..." she almost purred, unable to resist noticing how his plain black polo-top stretched across his chiselled torso. Feeling suddenly warm, she tossed the partially devoured pizza slice back into its box before grabbing one of the nearby bottles of mineral water, unscrewing the lid and taking a long swig, washing the last of the dry bread down. The water was refreshingly chilled, however it did little to ease the warmth that spread through her abdomen. "So who's your friend?" she asked after taking a second drink.

Daniel's eyebrow arched, giving her a swarthy but quizzical look that would have had Roger Moore green with envy. Suddenly unable to muster the words, her throat as coarse and dry as sandpaper, she nodded towards the door leading through to the foyer before taking another drink from the water bottle. He followed her gaze just in time to watch the beauty he'd been speaking with moments before slink out of the kitchen.

Someone obviously can't handle a little competition.

"Ooh, that's Monica. We were friends in school and were just catching up," he remarked in an innocent, offhanded tone that did not match the glint in his eyes.

"Yeah, if you say so..." Mina teased, her lips curling knowingly as she recalled how his eyes had been glued to the girl's generous cleavage. Seemingly unaffected by her departure however, he never so much as blinked an eye when his would-be conquest grabbed another reveller's arm in the hallway and proceeded to drag the stunned youth into the living room. "Well, she seems... *special.*"

Daniel turned to face her, and Mina felt her stomach tighten as his blue eyes looked into hers. Suddenly all traces of the boy she'd known so long ago were gone and instead, a man stood before her, wild and untamed with a fierce intensity in his gaze. For a moment, he was silent, but his eyes held her captive. He reached out to touch her cheek, his fingers rough against her softer skin. When he spoke, his voice was low and deep. "I'd forgotten just how beautiful you are."

The kitchen felt very warm. Her heart quickened and she opened her mouth to speak, but the words stuck in her throat and her voice trembled beneath his gaze. His head began to dip forward, closing the gap between them. He had a very nice mouth, Mina decided, perfectly shaped. Drawn to his lips, she edged forward, her eyes growing heavy as she inhaled his strong, masculine scent. He smelled of salt and sand.

A loud splash shattered the moment, followed by roars of laughter and a slurred curse. Mina's heart jumped into her throat and her head snapped round. One of the jugglers, a ruby-faced youth with short sandy hair and a squat build, had mistaken his drink for one of the empties, hurling it into the air only for it to turn end over end, spilling the amber contents upon his head. Drenched from head to toe, with his clothes clinging to him and beer running down his face in rivulets, he performed an exaggerated bow as the sight had his friends doubling over in fits of laughter.

"Oi!" Daniel barked, his voice bristling with such naked anger that all three went stiff as he moved past Mina with his white-knuckled fists clenched at his sides. The kitchen fell silent, the music playing in the living room fading into the background. At once, all eyes turned on Daniel. The floor and walls seemed to tremble beneath the heavy thump of each slow, purposeful stride.

His height dwarfed everyone around him and when he finally came to stand over the three, Mina's stomach tightened. She couldn't tell if it was with arousal or fear, or both.

"This is not a fucking frat party," he growled. His voice was low and he pronounced each word with deadly emphasis. "Now, I'm going to say this only once. If you want to clown around, then fuck off because I'll ram these cups down your throats if I see you pulling this kind of shit again." Coming to a stop barely a stride from them, he glared down at them, towering over the tallest by more than a foot. "Do I make myself clear?"

Only one, the drunkard dripping with beer and wearing a bemused grin, dared meet his gaze. He swayed slightly, shifted his weight between his feet, opened his mouth to speak, then lost his nerve as Daniel arched a brow. His hard eyes bore into the drunk kid's droopy sockets, and the youth turned his eyes down to the floor. All three nodded meekly.

He dismissed them with a curt sideways nod, sending all three bolting for the dining room, stumbling and tripping over each other in their haste to escape. Mina could barely keep her grin at bay as she watched them go. The ruby faced juggler fell flat on his face in the doorway and Mina glimpsed Daniel's hard expression suddenly blossom into a broad smile. The sight had her heart fluttering in her breast, like a bird soaring to the heavens.

Oh God, what am I doing? Her stomach wound into knots. *This is crazy! He's Mark's friend for fuck's sake!* The thought had her cheeks burning bright crimson. Forcing her attention back to the now, she found Daniel standing over her. Yet she saw only the mischievous-eyed boy. *Hmm... Interesting. Where did that come from?*

"W-well, that was... impressive." Her voice was shaky, her lips tingling with the ghost of the kiss that almost was. "So, what are you doing with yourself now? Do you have a girlfriend or... something?" she stammered, desperate to distract herself from the smouldering fire burning through her centre, the words flowing from her without much thought. Realising what she'd asked, Mina's cheeks burned all the fiercer and she took another draught from the almost empty bottle, hoping to drown in its clear depths.

Daniel's grin broadened, the muscles beneath his skin stretching the left corner of his mouth almost all the way back to his ear. Then the golden flecks in his eyes glinted, and he took the bottle from her hand, tipped his head back, and began to drink. Her breath caught in her throat as she watched, eyes wide and mouth hanging ajar, entranced by the subtle motions of his stubble-roughened throat, his jugular rising and falling each time he swallowed, draining the bottle.

Hopelessly entranced, it was only by pure chance she glimpsed him watching her through the clear plastic out of the corner of her eye. Like a deer in the headlights, Mina stood rigid, her feet rooted to the floor. She should have been embarrassed, ashamed of being caught staring at him so brazenly. Yet the look in his eyes, so full of mischief and zealous confidence, sent a tingling rush surging through her centre.

Get a grip, girl! You can do this.

She held his gaze regardless, forcing herself to don the calm, stoic mask she displayed during auditions, determined not to betray any hint of the effect he was having on her.

Screwing the lid onto the empty water bottle, Daniel tossed it over his shoulder into the half-full rubbish bin. A single drop of water rolled down his chin, but he brushed it away casually with the pad of his thumb. The gesture left a slick trail across his jaw that Mina longed to taste.

"It's girlfriends," he confirmed, his smirk never faltering. "And no. No, I'm not seeing anyone at the moment." His eyes peered down at her keenly, as if gauging her reaction, before he added, "Work doesn't really leave much time for relationships."

Despite herself, Mina couldn't help but raise a slender eyebrow. "Oh? And just what manner of nefarious employment is that, then, young Daniel?" she asked. Her lips curled in a small, playful smile. "The last time I saw you, you were going to become the next Batman. You would even run around the house wearing your mother's tights on your head for a cowl and cape. Did your dream come true? Is that it? Do you wander the dark city streets at night, fighting crime in a desperate quest to redeem yourself for how you tortured me as a child?"

"Not quite." Though he had the good grace to appear embarrassed, her remark left only a small, temporary dent in his cool composure. "Actually, I'm in the army."

"You're kidding!" There was no need for her to feign surprise. It was as genuine as her disbelief. Mina's eyes narrowed suspiciously and she watched him closely. Yet his expression was as genuine as any she had ever seen, those gold-speckled eyes gazing into hers, intense, never wavering. If he was playing her false, then he was a better actor than most of the A-listers in Hollywood. Nevertheless, Mina wasn't convinced. Deciding to play his game, she remarked, "Well, congratulations. And you just so happen to be out on parole for my little brother's party. How very *convenient*."

"Well, not exactly." He gave her an innocent look that did not show in his eyes. "I wasn't due any leave until June, but when I got Mark's message about this birthday bash, I had a word with the base's *XO* who owed me a favour, and voilà, here I stand." He spread his powerful arms, emphasising his presence.

"Hmmm..." It was only sheer force of will that kept her withering look at bay, his game quickly wearing Mina's patience. Yet he'd spoken easily, the words rolling off his silver tongue dripping with honey. *No lie!* "So the brass owes you favours?"

He dropped his hands back down to his sides and shrugged. "Sort of. His son went AWOL last year. After twenty days, I received a tip and found him in the pent-house of Hamburg's Kempinski Hotel with two hookers and a rather shaken goat. He was stoned out of his mind." He chuckled at the memory. "After confining him to the bar-racks, I had a private word with the Lieutenant Colonel. We made a deal. I agreed to report his son had voluntarily surrendered himself to me, and overlook his certain *indiscretions*, in exchange for him owing me a favour or two. I scratch his back, he scratches mine, as they say."

"A tip told you where to find an *XO*'s son?" she repeated slowly, her brow knitting with confusion, the mask hiding her beginning to crack. Something didn't feel right. No, it couldn't be true. He was lying, he had always been lying. But what if...

"Yeah. I'm in the MPs," he said, then added sourly, "It was a stupid decision, really. Crooked Nazi bastard could have had me arrested and on a charge of conduct unbecoming, dereliction of duty, and whatever other jumped-up charge he could make stick at any time. But I wagered he cared more about his career and the damage I could do to his prospects for promotion if word about his son's little misadventure were to slip. After all, top-class hotels have such excellent security records these days." However, Mina was no longer listening.

"The M... Ps..." Her throat was suddenly dry and there was a noticeable tremor in her voice as the words stuck there, the pit of her stomach plummeting. "You're really serious, aren't you? You're not joking."

His grumbling forgotten, Daniel gave her a half-smile. "Afraid so. Hmm... not quite what you expected?" She nodded meekly, unable to look him in the eye. "Well, I can't say I ever envisioned myself as Captain America either. The shield's a little cumbersome, but at least I don't have to wear tights."

Mina missed the joke. All at once, the world seemed to slip away into a roar of white noise at his words, and the inescapable implications coiled around them, hitting her like an icy wall of water, crashing over her head and down her spine to drive the bottom from the pit of her stomach. *It can't be... it just can't be...* At a loss, she could only stare up at him in incomprehension, watching him talk but hearing nothing. It couldn't be true. No, she just didn't want it to be true.

Daniel Cornwell had been Mark's best friend since preschool. Yet despite their friendship, they were as different as gold and onyx. Mark was wiry, pale, and utterly beyond reproach while Danny was broad, dark, sly, and as prone to mischief as a chimpanzee, a damn sprite who had taken every opportunity to tease and torment her. Any time Mark had gotten into trouble it was always a sure thing that little Danny Cornwell would be at the root of it. It was difficult to imagine the routine, duty, and order of a soldier's life appealing to that boy, never mind the Bow Street Runners. However, here he stood, and though her every instinct warned it was just another dirty trick he'd concocted to torment her, she believed him.

It was only when she felt the thrill of his gaze on her, raking over her naked skin through her clothes, that she realised he'd stopped talking. He loomed over her, his handsome face marred by a concerned expression that had his sexy lips pressed together in a tight frown, those mischievous gold-flecked eyes watching her with a note of concern.

Shit! Cursing inwardly, her cheeks grew hot under his gaze and she glanced away, avoiding meeting his eyes long enough to brush a wing of spun gold that had fallen out of place back behind her ear. "So... the military police huh...?" she forced herself to say. The words sounded strange to her, as though she were speaking another language for the first time, yet, whatever the tongue, the notion was no less ridiculous.

"I know. It's crazy, right?" Daniel said, visibly relaxing and giving a small shrug of his very broad shoulders. "But I guess you could say I was inspired. I read a lot of the Jack Reacher novels in school."

"And you're enjoying it?" she asked awkwardly, unsure of what else to say, so giving voice to the first thought that occurred to her. "I-I mean you're only this young once. Are you sure this is what you want to do with your life?"

"Jeez, relax, *mum*," he laughed, rolling his eyes in a mocking gesture. "It's not a career choice. I just want to do my bit, see the world, and score whatever points I can for myself along the way."

In the living room a raucous cheer rose from the revellers as the music switched to a more popular song Mina still didn't know. Daniel, meanwhile, appeared not to notice and instead developed a thoughtful look. "Though I suppose it could be something of a family trade now. Dad joined up when he was my age and Gramps was in the first wave on Omaha Beach. They enjoyed their time serving Uncle Sam, so when I dropped out of school, I thought why not? It beats flipping burgers at McDonald's. So I signed my life away. Next thing I know, I'm out of boot and being shipped off to Germany."

Mina couldn't help but giggle playfully. He might very well be the sprite of memory, but in one thing he had not changed. He had a knack for making her laugh. "Well, I don't know about Jack Reacher. Your life sounds more like the makings of a John Grisham novel. Blackmail, corruption- you should become an agent. Mine's considering taking on a partner if you want me to put in a word for you."

"I'll keep that in mind." When he smiled, it was like the sun was breaking across the horizon and Mina felt her heart flutter against its cage as a bird would beat its wings.

What is he doing to me?

"So what about you? I hear you're seeing that Jason Stoker from *Insurrection*," he remarked, referring to the box office flop Jason had starred in. It had been released worldwide in December but had also been widely condemned. "Are things... good between the two of you?" Was that concern she heard, or mocking?

"Yeah, we're fine," she said with an offhanded twist to her lips. "We just moved in together last August, but how do you know about that? I don't recall adding you on Facebook." Mina's eyes narrowed suspiciously.

While she was hardly discreet, she never talked to the media about her personal life, publicly or off the record. As far as she was concerned, there was an invisible line dividing her career and her private life, and she never crossed it. Her Facebook account was one of the few places she posted intimate details, but to a contacts list consisting of around thirty of her closest friends and family. Unlike her Twitter profile, where she had over five hundred thousand followers, used solely to prank fellow celebrities. Orlando Bloom still hadn't forgiven her for a little Photoshop experiment she'd pulled just before the premiere of *Pirates of the Caribbean 5*, and Justin Bieber had tried to get a restraining order against her IP address.

"Are you stalking me?" It was only half a joke. *He is a soldier, after all, and an MP besides. Who knows what strings he can pull?*

Daniel chuckled. "You got me. I hack into your webcam every night to watch you get done-up in Kate Beckinsale's leather bodysuit and whip your little piggy." His guffaw fell silent when he caught sight of the warning in her eyes. "No. I read a few articles in *Dirt Roundup* that had some paparazzi snapshots of the two of you walking hand-in-hand along the Santa Monica Pier before going to dinner at Cavatina. You know he's gay, right?"

"What! Jason's not-"

"So this is the sister we've all heard so much about," a sly voice announced from across the kitchen. Her outburst died on her lips and Mina wheeled towards the source of the interruption to find four young men arrayed in a thin line, blocking the door leading through to the foyer. They all grinned wickedly and a shiver crept down her spine as she realised they all had their eyes on her. The one on the far left took an extra step forward to stand centre stage. Recognising his flaming hair, Mina realised these were the boys whom she'd encountered standing on the doorstep.

"Well?" he asked. "Come on, Daniel, where are your manners? Introduce us."

His easy smile finally faltered and Daniel's lips pursed into a thin line as his eyes darted nervously towards her. But before she could ask what was wrong, he stepped into the space dividing her from them and swept out a hand towards the speaker.

"Mina, this is Sean." Despite his broad grin and runner's build, Mina couldn't help but think that his beady eyes, flaming red hair and flat, stubby nose gave Sean the face of a ferret. Oblivious to her thoughts, Daniel was already gesturing to the remaining members of the group. "Eric," he said, pointing towards a round-faced, pockmarked boy with listless brown hair, skin the colour of curdled milk, and dull green eyes, who stood at least a foot shorter than the rest. "Charlie," who was a lean-figured male who appeared older than his years due to shoulder-length silver-blond hair, a stubble-roughened chin, and clever grey irises. "And this imposing brute is Victor." Victor was the most striking of the lot. A broad, heavily muscled bruiser who dwarfed anyone in his shadow, who must have spent five hours a day in the gym and shaved his head twice a week to have his pate as smooth as marble.

Together they made an imposing, yet comical band of misfits. "They were in Mark's and my homeroom in high school." Daniel then waved his hand back towards her. "*Gentleman*," he sullenly muttered the word like a cobra spitting venom. "This is Mark's stepsister, Mina Carring."

Forcing a friendly smile, Mina raised an open-palmed hand in greeting. "Hi." None of them made any move to respond and instead, they just watched her, their eyes gleaming with predatory hunger. Her smile faded and the hand fell back to her side. "I'm not staying long, I just dropped by to wish Mark a happy birthday."

Thin, gaunt-faced Charlie sniggered and gestured back over his shoulder towards the stairs in the foyer. "You just missed him," he said. "He went up to his room about fifteen minutes ago. Had a little accident with his beer."

"Thanks." Nodding, Mina twisted back to Daniel and gave him a small smile. "Well, it was good to see you again, Danny." He looked like he was about to say something, but she interceded him by leaning up on tiptoes and kissed him softly on the cheek. Then, spinning on her heel, she darted between Victor and Eric, and walked briskly down the hall. She narrowly avoided barrelling into a startled boy carrying two cups of beer in each hand as she bolted up the sweeping stairs, taking the shallow steps three at a time.

What was all that about? she wondered, thinking back to the encounter in the kitchen and the change that had come over Daniel. A shudder crept down her spine. She couldn't explain it, but upon seeing him standing on the porch, she'd taken an instant disliking to Sean.

It's his eyes.

When he looked at her, they sat in their sockets like bergs floating on the ocean- cold and blue and only hinting at a danger lurking beneath the surface. And there was something else, a sort of madness that had nothing to do with the effects of the drugs. Did Daniel have some sort of history with Sean and those three other clowns? If so, then it was a sure thing that Mark had an equal share in it. So what were they doing here?

Despite the hive of activity and commotion below, the house's second floor landing was utterly deserted. Turning left at the top of the stairs, the soft carpet underfoot and the deep thunder of the party below muffling her steps, she swept down the dim, narrow passage, passing the door of her old room on her left and two others on her right. Stopping outside Mark's door, the last on the left, she raised a hand to kno-

What was that?

The sound was small, barely more than a whisper, yet it struck a chord that had Mina suddenly still as stone. There it was again, the whisper of a voice, too faint to understand but recognisable all the same.

He can't be.

Dropping her hand to her side, Mina sank to her knees and pressed her ear against the door, straining to hear over the ruckus going on downstairs.

A puckish smirk turned the corner of her full rosy lips.

He is!

Three

 Grasping the handle, she tried the lever and found the door unlocked. Mina said a silent prayer for someone to have finally fixed the old squeak and gave it a gentle nudge. Without a sound, the door slid inward and edging slightly forward, Mina peered through the crack.

Oh my!

The room was dark and dim. What light there was came off the small lamp on the bedside table, a soft golden luminance that enhanced the gloom and made the furniture appear surreal and shapeless amongst the shadows. Mark was half sitting, half lying upon his bed with his back propped against the woven metalwork headboard, naked and vigorously stroking his stiff length.

Mina licked her lips, her heartbeat rising to a thunderous storm within her breast as her greedy azure eyes devoured the voyeur's feast laid before her, memorising every detail. University life had certainly seemed to agree with him. Where once he'd been boyishly spindly, he'd grown limber with long, well-defined legs and a firm abdomen just hinting to the rippling muscles beneath his milky skin. Her knees began to quake and tremble.

By the look of him he had just come from the shower. His hair was still damp and half plastered to his face while drops of moisture glistened across his torso, rolling down his skin and sparkling like diamonds when they caught the light. Entranced by the slow roll of liquid, her eyes were drawn to a single fat drop that slithered down the flat of his abdomen until it vanished within a nestle of dark curls. Her gaze settled on his hard length and she had to bite her lip to rein in her low, wanton moan.

Only the head remained permanently in view, a swollen, purple-grey bell shining with a thick sheen of pre-cum and pulsing so vividly it was a wonder it hadn't already burst beneath his attention. Oblivious to his audience, Mark's hand slid up and down the shaft, his motions swift, purposeful, and very well practised. His breathing was low and urgent, coming in short pants punctuated by the occasional low groan, like a great snorting beast preparing to charge. With each stroke, his fingers flexed around the length of his shaft, tightening and loosening, simulating the muscular convulsions of his fantasy lover, causing fresh droplets of glistening syrup to form on the tip.

He must be in a hurry, she realised breathlessly, *probably hoping to finish and be back at the party before anyone realises he's gone.*

Drinking in the sight of his hand pumping up and down in that urgent rhythm, Mina's mouth began to water. Accustomed as she was to the sight of male nakedness, there was something so erotic, so deliciously taboo about spying on him, watching him indulge in this most private of moments. At the apex of each stroke, a spike pulsed through her centre. She was suddenly very aware of the liquid heat that exploded through her centre and of the dampness seeping through the crotch of her jeans.

She needed to go, a part of her suddenly urged. Now was not the time for these games. It was too dangerous. There were too many people, and should one of them venture up the stairs and discover her... The consequences didn't bear thinking about. Besides, they'd agreed these dalliances had to stop. They had both agreed. Yet the risk, that thrill of seeing how far they could push the boundaries and the ever-present danger of discovery that loomed over them, had always made their games so much more exciting.

I need to...

A haze was amassing, shrouding her thoughts, making it difficult to think as desire's liquid heat ran molten through her veins, fanning the smouldering embers in her core until they erupted in a raging inferno.

I need to...

The thought danced in and out of her comprehension but was quickly little more than a distant memory lying just beyond her grasp.

I need...

Her plush inner walls responded to his motions, clenching around a phantom cock in time with his strokes while her clit swelled with arousal, its need for contact growing almost unbearable.

I need...

Bit by bit, her hand began to slip beneath her jeans...

"Oh- ffuck... Mina!"

Mina froze as her heart leapt into her throat at the familiar call. Reality returned in an icy wash that cascaded down her spine. Dragging her eyes from his shaft, she hauled her eyes up to where she expected to meet his startled gaze, only he wasn't looking towards her. In fact, he hadn't noticed her at all. His narrow face was leaner, almost gaunt, but also older, yet with the same soft features and floppy mop of hair that almost masked half his face. Hidden beneath the wispy strands of dark chestnut, his chocolate eyes never wavered from a small glossy rectangle of photo paper Mina hadn't noticed before, cradled in his left hand, the quickening rise and fall of his stomach obscuring it from her view.

"Mina... ugh fuck... so tight..." he grunted, in a voice little more than a whisper. "So tight... I love it!"

It was at the wrong angle for her to make out clearly. However, possessed by a sudden insurmountable curiosity that had a mass of moths fluttering through her insides, she squinted and tilted her head from side to side, trying in vain to get a better view. As if he sensed her silent plea, the hand grasping the photo tilted ever so slightly towards her. Mina's eyes widened. The photo was of her.

The little weasel was jerking off to a picture of her! The realisation sent a hot tremor down her spine that got her long legs quaking, the teasers of a mini-orgasm echoing out from her centre. Well, she'd have to put a stop to that.

Clambering to her feet, Mina quickly composed herself. Feeling the same nervous thrill she always experienced on the first day of filming, she took a calming breath and glanced back over her shoulder to check that the hall was still clear of spectators, before she slipped into character and gave the door a nudge. It swung inward to emit a satisfying crack against the wall. Stepping inside and flicking on the light switch, the actress proclaimed, "Well... well... well... what have we here?"

Bright, brilliant luminance flooded the room, banishing the shadows. Thrown into sharp contrast, Mark's room appeared just as she'd remembered it from her last visit. Glossy skinned maxi-posters bedecked every wall. An Ikea corner desk, stashed away in the near corner, was strewn with rings of hard-backed textbooks arranged around her stepbrother's prized Alienware laptop. The sofa he'd inherited from his grandmother sat opposite an entertainment centre about ready to collapse beneath the treasure trove of devices burdening its many tiered shelves.

Only his overnight bag, lying half-open on the floor, gave any indication Mark was only home for a few days. Clothes, damp with something that looked suspiciously like beer, were scattered around the holdall. *A little accident indeed*, she thought coldly, remembering Charlie's snigger.

But just what sort of accident?

Bolting upright, torn so rudely from the arms of his fantasy, Mark immediately seized one of the pillows to cover himself. He looked like a rabbit caught in a trap. Upon seeing it was Mina who'd discovered him, however, he visibly relaxed, but couldn't meet her gaze as his normally pale complexion turned a vivid shade of pink. "Mina... what are you... no... how did you... I... I swear... this... this isn't what it looks like..."

How original.

"Oh? Is it not?" she asked coyly, cocking her head to the side and fixing him with a pondering stare. There was a soft *thump* as the door slid closed behind her under its own momentum. "You know, I'd expected something less cliché. Though I have to admit, I'd also thought you would know that, if you must sneak off in the middle of your own party to give yourself a treat, lock the bloody door!"

Never taking her eyes off him, Mina reached back and turned the locking mechanism, the bolt slamming into place with a reassuring *click*. Then, with all the predatory grace of a lioness stalking a mouse, she advanced towards the bed with deliberate slowness.

A bright splash of colour stained his cheeks as Mark looked down at his floor where his towel, still sodden from his shower, lay discarded and Mina had to resist the urge to giggle. He was so cute when he was embarrassed.

Coming to stand over him, she snatched the photo from his grasp. "What's this?"

"It's nothing!" His head flew up and he tried to grab it back but the motion proved too difficult while still pressing the pillow to his person and instead, almost toppled to the floor. Smirking, his stepsister sidestepped his desperate lunge and raised the snapshot into the light.

It was indeed a photo of her, taken two years before when she'd treated Mark to a week's holiday in Cyprus. It showed her reclining back on a deserted stretch of sandy beach in nothing but a white, close-fitting swimsuit, her skin glowing gold in the late afternoon sun and head tilted away from the camera towards the horizon. He'd probably kept it hidden away in his underwear draw, and stumbled upon it.

"Well, at least this means you're no longer stealing my panties," she said matter-of-factly, causing Mark's face to burn such a shade of red she wondered if he was about to cry with sheer embarrassment. Deciding to take pity on him, she casually threw the photo over her shoulder.

"Now, little brother." She shrugged off her jacket and let it fall around her feet before carefully stepping out of her boots. "Do you remember what I said the last time I walked in on you?" Slowly, ever so slowly, Mark looked up from his feet to meet her gaze, his eyes wide and questioning, and there was something else. Hope. There was hope there, but also uncertainty, as though he didn't dare believe what was happening for fear that it was all too good to be true. Mina understood his hesitancy. After all, they had both agreed never again, but damn it, she didn't care. She wanted him. Wanted him as she had never wanted any man before.

Holding his gaze, Mina slowly sat beside him on the edge of the bed. As she reached out to place a delicate hand upon his knee, she could barely rein in her victorious grin. The touch was light, gentle, almost cautious, but even so, Mark's back went as stiff as a board. Hard muscles rippled beneath warm skin, tensing at her touch. She pretended not to notice the way his eyes glanced downwards to watch her hand as though it were a venomous insect and she innocently tilted her head.

Keeping her movements soft and slow, so *tortuously* slow, she slid the offending hand higher. His flesh was hot against her fingers, the muscles beneath harder than she had expected. As she moved higher up his thigh, she could feel the tension amassing. A playful smile pulled at the corner of her lips.

"But what about..." His jaw was tight and what was left of his voice in that choked squeak gave out when her hand paused just below the pillow. Still endeavouring to resist her however, his hand began to shake, his knuckles turning bone-white as he pressed the pillow firmly to his groin. Her smile grew ever more coy and she raised her palm and swept her fingertips over his skin, drawing swirling feather-light patterns over the skin of his inner-thigh, just skirting the boundary of the pillow.

"If you want me to make you cum..."

She pivoted, swinging a long, perfectly toned leg across his waist, straddling him, barring escape and bringing them nose to nose. Leaning to the side, she ever so softly brushed her lips over his in the barest hint of a kiss, inwardly smirking as she felt him subtly shift to try and meet her, before mimicking the motions of the hand upon his thigh with the tip of her nose, sketching an intricate weaving web across his flushed cheek. She could feel his breath quicken, growing short and frayed, the warmth of each washing over her neck and sending tingling sensations shooting down her spine to the wet heat pulsing between her thighs. When her lips came within a hair's breadth of his ear, she whispered in a voice threaded with promise.

"...just ask."

The look in his eyes when she drew back made her feel like a cat toying with a mouse, glorying in the sweet ambrosia of holding such power over another living creature, just before it pounced.

"Mina..." Mark gulped, his tongue darting out to moisten his lips. "We shouldn't..."

Welding her full lips to his and thrusting her tongue into the warm cavern beyond, Mina silenced him with a hungry open-mouthed kiss. She didn't want to hear what they should or shouldn't do. She only wanted him and abandoning her teasing ministrations upon his thigh, Mina snatched the pillow from his grasp and cast it aside before she fisted her hand in his hair, the strands of dark chocolate softer than sable. Her free hand rose to cradle his jaw, the roughness of his skin rasping her palm and arousing her all the more as she swept her tongue in long circuits around his mouth and over his teeth, coaxing his own to dance.

Mark groaned an indeterminable sound, the deep resonance reverberating through his throat to tingle over her lips. Accepting the embrace, his arms encircled her narrow waist to paw wantonly at her full rump as he tried desperately to draw her closer whilst she cradled his head in her palms. He yielded without a struggle, their tongues thrusting, twisting, swirling around and around in a passionate dance before a low moan rumbled through her. Mina felt his renewed erection prod her thigh through her jeans. Feeling her core grow moist at the touch, she snaked her hand down his neck, her nails scraping over his flat nipples and down his torso before moving lower, the warm flesh of his stomach trembling beneath her fingers as she reached between their bodies. Coiling her digits around the base of his manhood while rubbing her palm across the glistening tip, she gave him a testing stroke. His hips bucked into her hand and he broke their burning embrace to drag in a ragged breath.

"Mmm... such a naughty boy..." she purred, slightly breathless from the kiss but smirking playfully nonetheless as she leaned back, settling herself above him. Within her grasp, his shaft was like a column of steel wrapped in molten silk and though he was well within average parameters, in her small hand he felt huge. She could feel him throb with excitement as blood surged through the bulging veins. Mina gave it a shake before stroking along his length from base to heap, stretching the velvety skin tight before completing each stroke with a firm squeeze just beneath the swollen lip of his corona that made the bulbous head swell. "Getting this hard from thinking about your stepsister. So do you want big sis to make you cum?"

"Yes..." he hissed through gritted teeth, his eyes wide and breath shallow as her talented hand continued it's ministrations, his hips jumping in sheer delight as she pressed the pad of her thumb upon the sensitised head.

Mina smirked wickedly, enjoying his look of desperation before releasing his shaft. With his relief nearing, Mark made a furious sound of protest but she paid it no mind as she got to her feet, turned around to face the foot of the bed and then sat back down. Kneeling over his waist, she then shuffled back until she was literally crouching over the length of his body with her head just above his abdomen and presenting him with her denim-clad buttocks.

Placing her hands on his inner thighs, she massaged the supple muscles with her palms and cast her gaze down to see his rampant erection standing proudly to attention, jutting over his chiselled thighs. Ropy veins bulged along the distended trunk and the mushroom-shaped crown glistened with precum. Up this close, it seemed bigger than she remembered and the musky scent of his arousal made her mouth water as she dipped her head and brought her lips close enough for the warmth of her breath to wash over his sturdy length.

"Ah..." he gasped and she could feel him tremble with pleasure, his engorged shaft twitching in excitement. Encouraged by his display, she reached out with her tongue and used the tip to skilfully scribble her signature across the organ's glans before she dragged it up to the weeping point, dousing her taste buds in his flavour. Relishing the familiar salty tang of male excitement, she flicked her tongue over the slick summit before she almost wrapped it around the bulbous head, slowly taking him into the damp cavern of her mouth. Closing her lips over the head, she began to earnestly suck the slick rubbery flesh while her tongue continued to swirl around and around, down to the sensitised ridges along its rim, making him shudder with pleasure.

With every sweeping crease and wanton suckle, his flesh pulsed within her grasp and she half heard him groan something incomprehensible, his voice low and laboured as her tongue danced. She noticed the tension that gathered in his thighs as he resisted the urge to buck, so she decided to take pity on him and slowly took him deeper. Her pouting lips stretched and formed a tight seal around his shaft as she leisurely leant forward, enveloping all but the last inch of him in her mouth. It was a necessary evil to avoid her persistent gag reflex. Even so, he filled her tiny orifice completely and she was forced to breathe through her nose as she held him in her mouth.

"Oh... fuck... fuck... Mina!" gasped Mark, his breath catching in his throat as she eagerly began to suckle the length of his arousal, drawing back and rising up at a tortuously slow pace until she held just the bulbous crown between her pearly whites. The salty taste of his arousal flooded her senses and she repeated the motion, dipping down while gently scraping her teeth along his engorged length before she rose up again, all the while sucking vigorously. The sounds of his pleasure sent hot shivers rushing all the way down her spine to spark deliciously within her molten sheath.

She had always loved performing oral sex. She had relished the power it gave her and the control she could wield over another person with just the tiniest motion of her mouth and tongue. It was so empowering and utterly addictive, but for all her bravado there was something she wanted even more.

She could feel the need burning deep within her, a fire that seemed to originate within her clit and rage outward along her nerves to keep her ever on edge. Mina fidgeted restlessly as slick rivulets of her dew rolled down her thighs, and she knew she needed her own release, so she suddenly ceased her attention. Pulling her mouth off his now glistening shaft, she flashed a look back over her shoulder at him, a sly smirk pulling at her lips as she saw his eyes squeeze tightly shut and a pleasurable grimace contort his handsome features. His hands had a white-knuckled death grip on the sheets and she could hear his breathing come in short, ragged gasps.

Perfect.

"Hey squirt, instead of just lying there, gibbering like a codfish, why don't you put that mouth to proper use and eat me? Sucking your dick is making me so wet..."

Unscrewing his eyes, he stared at her incredulously as she wiggled her butt provocatively, clearly not daring to believe what she had suggested, before nodding excitedly, reaching up and fumbling with the button of her jeans. For a moment he was all thumbs, but then managed to release the fastening and, hooking his fingers under the waistband, dragged the denim down.

She shivered as the cool air touched her most sensitive spots, contrasting so deliciously with the heat of her desire, before the warmth of Mark's breath was suddenly washing over her folds. His hands seized the full globes of her buttocks and dragged her down to his waiting jaws, his tongue slithering out to lap along her core. Parting but never entering her folds, he teased her with three long, gentle licks before finally thrusting into her depths. Her skin prickled with goose flesh and a low, sensuous moan echoed from her lips as she felt the thick muscle, slick from a manic lust, writhe inside her, spiralling, thrashing her quivering walls and feasting upon her syrupy dew. He devoured her with such a ravenous frenzy that she could not help but tighten her grip on his thighs and roll her hips against his tongue.

"Mmm... you naughty boy... oh... yes you dirty, naughty boy..." she moaned, as Mark's tongue orally fucked her. Although the pleasure this treat provided wasn't spectacular, he was doing so much better than the last time. Mina knew he must have been practising. Strangely, the thought of him doing this to some other girl filled her with a momentary surge of anger. A sudden, and very delightful, swirl of his tongue quickly buried her thoughts and lavished her folds with attention, avoiding any contact with her sensitised clitoris. He began to withdraw and then thrust back into her tight passage, greedily lapping up her flowing nectar. She felt a surge of emotion and such a rush of pleasure that it seemed to set every nerve in her body ablaze.

Exhaling hot panting breaths but determined not to be outdone, Mina wasted no time getting back to work on him. Taking him in her mouth once again, she swirled her tongue around his crown, synchronizing her motions with his assault as she resumed bobbing back and forth, sliding her lips along his hard length, continuing to use her teeth to apply a gentle pressure. It was difficult work for his wicked tongue was stirring up a storm within her and it took all of her concentration to push the feeling of him writhing within her to the back of her mind, ignoring it as she would that itch you could never quite scratch.

Vaguely she heard him drag in a ragged breath and she could feel his muscles flex excitedly beneath her palms. He suddenly started to buck and roll beneath her, forcing his rampant arousal a little deeper down her throat as he moved to meet her descent. Anticipating the kick of her gag reflex, fear blossomed in her heart and she panicked, trying desperately to withdraw and breathe only to feel a sudden scorching bolt of white-hot ecstasy rip through her, stilling her as Mark's devious techniques altered.

With supreme confidence unsuitable for a man caught masturbating to a picture of his step sister, he began to worship the core of her erogenous being with swift licks and prods. Frozen in a wash of tiny climactic aftershocks, her world shrank to just the sensation of his tongue circling her engorged clit, her every sense focused entirely on the fiery kisses that flamed her entire being. In such a delirious state as this, the sensation seemed to last for an eternity, but was then shattered as a barrage of fireworks burst behind her eyes as his lips closed on her sensitised nub.

Fire ran through her veins and her body jumped with the mini-teasers of an orgasm, yet his fingers held her firm against him as he pressed the tip of his nose inside her while fiercely suckling the tiny bud. Pulse after pulse of insidious bliss surged along her nerves, throwing her into such a state of delirium that she couldn't hold back a wanton chorus of delight, her voice reverberating through his shaft in such a way that she felt him shudder in pleasure and growl around her bud. The sensations were so divine that her back arched on its own accord, yanking her suddenly clear of his cock and she moaned her pleasure without thought or care, heedless of anyone who might overhear them at that very moment. "Oh... right there. Right... ugh... yes, suck that clit. Ugh holy fuck! Oh- my-God- oh- my- God..."

Her heart was thundering in her ears as her vision dissolved into a collage of vivid colours, and she forced herself to recover and resume working on him. Barely able to think through the storm of pleasure clouding her mind, she was determined not to be out done. She focused all of her attention on bobbing up and down on his cock while massaging the glans across the domed head with her tongue. Relishing the bittersweet flavour that spilled across her taste buds, she began to earnestly suck the organ, earning a low, pleasure-induced hum from Mark that had her body backing into him and rocking against his ravenous lips.

It wouldn't be long now. She could feel her muscles clench and there was an unmistakable tightness building in her lower abdomen that could only foretell a much-needed climax. Judging by the way his shaft was pulsing between her lips, she knew Mark must have been close too, but despite her best efforts, she was certain she would reach that glorious peak before him. Deciding it was time to break out the heavy calibres and try something unconventional, she edged her right palm along his thigh to cup the weight of his balls in her hand. Mina gently kneaded the velvety sack while raising her left up to her lips, coating the digits in copious amounts of saliva. When sufficiently lubricated, she reached down and trailed the glistening point of her index finger's nail along the soft skin of his perineum to his anus. Noticing how his cock seemed to grow harder and thicker between her lips, she grinned inwardly before she pressed against the puckered sphincter. Mark's body jumped at the forbidden contact before going suddenly still as she slid the well-lubricated finger through the two tight rings of muscle into his anal channel.

Going just past her second knuckle, she then curled the digit and began exploring the dry, spongy walls until she felt the bumpy mound of his prostate.

"Ahh... Mina!" Mark gasped as she pressed down on the gland. His anal channel clenched tightly around her finger and he spilled his molten seed into her mouth. Thrilled by his salty essence, she suckled greedily, swallowing every drop of his release as he writhed beneath her in a fit of euphoria. Mark accidentally scraped the chiseled edge of his incisors across her clit as he threw his head back and arched off the bed. A sudden volatile cocktail of pleasure and pain flared through her at the contact, pitching her over the edge. Indescribable sensations of pleasure surged through her, originating from the lightning raging within her clitoris and pulsing deliciously through her every nerve until her mind was consumed by her release. At its crescendo, everything became too much. Her eyes squeezed shut, and she could feel herself shake violently as all notions of time and space slipped away. She hung there in limbo, poised between consciousness and oblivion, suspended in a heavenly sea of euphoria before plummeting back down to earth to ride the current of aftershocks.

Her skin tingled as she came slowly down from her high. Blinking past the fog of delirium, she felt Mark relax beneath her and quickly swallowed the last of his seed before withdrawing her finger from his tight anus. Releasing his balls and easing her mouth off his still-hard length, she reared back and sat straight-backed astride his torso. Her legs wobbled dangerously, barely able to support her weight, and she almost jumped out of her skin when Mark's tongue resumed licking her, making slow, languishing sweeps along her folds, scooping up her dew like drops off a slowly melting ice-lolly.

Extremely sensitive after such an intense climax, she couldn't help but exhale hot wanton pants as each gentle crease made her sensitised clit throb with need. She forced her body to move. Rising up, if somewhat unsteadily, she stepped out of her jeans and kicked them across the room before she threw a leg over his torso, pivoted, and came around to face him. Seeing the confusion in his expression, she flashed him a coy smile before crouching over his eager erection.

"Mmmm... that was fun but now just sit back and enjoy the rest of your present Squirt, because big sis is about to rock your world," she said before brushing a long strand of her rich blond hair that had fallen astray back behind her ear. Holding herself above his stiff manhood and balancing on the balls of her feet, she placed her left palm flat upon his abdomen to steady herself and reached down between them with her right. Wrapping her fingers around his arousal to position him, she lowered herself until she felt his rounded head slip between her folds. Compared to the heat boiling within her, Mark's shaft felt positively chilled and she shivered with pleasure as he pressed against her opening. She rolled her hips, sliding the sensitive tip along her hidden valley to brush the nub of her clitoris, sending a jolt of sensations surging along her nerves.

Biting her lower lip in pleasure, she rocked back and forth, caressing him with her velvety furrow and coating the mushroom-shaped crown with her hot nectar, all the while smirking as she watched him squirm beneath her, her every motion eliciting a desperate sound in response. Yet like a good boy, he followed her instructions and made no effort to interfere or hasten her, leaving Mina free to tease him until the fiery passion raging within her core grew too great to resist. Eager to continue and almost trembling with pent-up passion, she rocked forward...

"Oh!" she moaned, her head rolling back in utter delight as she felt the first delicious shock of penetration surge through her when the bulbous head of her stepbrother's cock drove through the tight ring of muscle into her channel. Her breath caught at the sudden wash of pleasure that radiated through her lower body and she released her grip on him. She placed her palm on his abdomen before leaning back, mewing as her inner walls stretched to accommodate him, moulding around inch after wondrous inch until he was sheathed to the hilt within her.

She held herself there, savouring the sensation of having him inside her. While he certainly wasn't the biggest she'd ever had, the feeling was very pleasurable and just the thought that it was her stepbrother's cock buried inside her sent a naughty thrill tingling down her spine to her fingertips. Impaled as she was, she could feel her plush walls pulse deliciously in time with her heartbeat, convulsing around him in such a way that her whole centre began to throb with desire. Suddenly unsure of how long she could hold herself in check, her head dropped down to admire the image of Mark splayed beneath her. Though he had not moved once, he clutched the sheets in a white-knuckled hold once more and his lips were pulled tight in a grimace as his restraint was strained to its limit.

As their eyes locked, she gave him a reassuring wink before gently biting her lower lip as she resumed rolling her pelvis in tight little circles, massaging his engorged length with her velvety walls. Though her motions were slow and gentle, she was a well-practised dominator and the pleasure it gave her was enough to throw her senses into overdrive, feeding her need and making her skin prickle with electricity. Rocking back and forth, she ground their hips together, her muscles contracting around him at the delicious friction between their bodies and sending pulses of white-hot pleasure surging up her spine.

"Aah! God! Mina…" panted Mark, his breathing laboured and pupils constricting to pinpoints under the strain of keeping still. "Feels so-so… good, I have to…"

"Mmm… like that, baby? Want big sister to ride you harder?" Mina asked, barely able to keep her composure as the fires raged within her core, rising with each roll of her hips. Bit by bit, she could feel her pleasure building, and carried by the surge of sensations, she began to pick up the pace, pushing up with her feet until she had just the rounded head inside her depths, leaving her feeling almost empty, before slamming back down. As she settled upon him, the tempting heat caused Mark to groan a low, desperate sound and his hands seized her full buttocks as his knees bent on their own volition.

They moaned in unison as the new angle pushed his shaft deeper inside her, but Mina never lingered and continued moving along his length. Keeping her eyes fixed to Mark's lust-darkened orbs, relishing the sight of him contorting in such pleasurable agony, she slid up and down, working his rigid cock in and out of her tight pussy. With each deep plunge, soft moans fled her lips and her pace quickened, until the bedsprings were creaking with her movements as she bounced upon him.

Beneath her, Mark was panting through clenched teeth, uttering low moans every time he was fully encased inside her, his fingers groping and kneading the tight mounds of her buttocks, his trimmed nails digging in just hard enough for her to feel the sting and know he was leaving small half-moon marks.

"Ooh... like that, baby? Mmm- you like watching your sister bounce on your cock, don't you? Yeah, I know you do. It feels so fucking good..." she purred, the sensation of his cock stretching and rubbing against her inner walls as she gyrated upon him, sending hot shivers rushing up her spine. With her every move she could feel that familiar pressure mounting inside her, a low burning pleasure amassing at the base of her spine, and she struggled to keep her motions fluid. Yet her body needed more, and on the next downward plunge, her hips rolled subtly to rub her G-spot along his length.

The sudden jolt had her hands pawing the flat plane of her sibling's stomach and her mouth fell open in a long moan. Sensing her muscles tense around him, drawing him deeper into her depths, she couldn't help but tilt her hips so that every stroke would brush that sweet spot.

"Ahh... ahh... God! It's... it's so hot... ugh... so... hot!" Mina moaned, her core dissolving into a pit of molten wildfire and sending a rush of warmth coursing through her veins. Swept along on the furious tide of her orgasm, she could no longer hold herself back and began bounding up and down with renewed vigour. It was getting harder for her to breathe, her lungs squashed by the constricting hold of her top, the cotton growing tighter by the second. No! It was too tight! So hot! She needed to breathe. Her back arching, she raked her hands down Mark's flat abdomen and up her thighs to where the hem of her top clung to her midriff. Seizing the garment in both hands, she dragged it up her body, breaking eye contact for the first time as she pulled it up and over her head in one effortless motion before carelessly flinging it off the bed to the floor, leaving her utterly naked. Mark's gaze immediately fixed on her cleavage.

Typical.

The air felt chilled and her skin prickled under his hungry gaze. The feeling of cool air wafting over her fevered flesh served only to make the fires burn fiercer. She brought both her hands up to cup her perky breasts, expertly kneading the pliant flesh while rolling her already pebbled nipples between her thumb and forefingers. She was so sensitive at that moment that even the lightest touch was electric, and she arched wantonly into her own touch, trying to receive more of the pleasure shooting through her body.

The sight of her shamelessly groping her breasts while riding him however, proved too much for Mark and he instinctively bucked up to meet her downward motion.

"Ah!" she gasped, tossing her head back in sheer ecstasy as his sudden forcefulness drove him deeper, her walls stretching and rippling around him, sparks of pleasure igniting behind her eyes. Caught off guard, her legs gave way and she had to throw her arms out as she doubled over in rapture. Bracing her palms against his shoulders, nails biting into his skin, she tried to gather enough breath to scold him for his disobedience but he was well past caring and with a primal grunt, began thrusting upward into her liquid heat.

"Ugh! Mina... your pussy's so small, so tight... I love it!" he gasped, his eyes alive with feral lust, driving into her with desperate, almost mindless strokes. The sound of Mark's voice saying such dirty things gave her a naughty thrill, and he was being so rough with each thrust she could feel the fire in her loins spread as her channel pulsed, sending bolts of white-hot desire travelling along her nerves. Forgetting her objections, Mina gave herself up to his powerful thrusts.

Moving with him, matching him thrust for deep, penetrating thrust, she rocked and rolled her hips, bouncing vigorously upon his shaft, filling the space between them with the wet slaps of flesh meeting flesh as her nectar ran down her thighs. Delighting in her exuberance, Mark rocked and thrashed and groaned beneath her, his forceful lunges delving ever deeper into her plush depths as her eager hips gyrated, riding him with increasing fervour.

"Oh... you bad boy... ah... ah- yes... you like your stepsister bouncing up and down on your dick? Mmm... want me to fuck you harder- oh... God... your dick feels so go... oh... God!" she moaned, damp strands of her rich golden hair spilling over her shoulder as she rose and fell upon him, her mind consumed by his hard length filling her, then retreating, only to fill her again.

Releasing her grip on his shoulders as white-capped waves crashed over her at his every thrust, she stretched her hands out across the rumpled sheets to seize the headboard, using it for leverage to roll her hips against his with greater urgency. Hovering over the curve of his neck, panting hot, wanton breaths as the inferno raging in her core burned with fresh intensity, signifying her building climax, she bent down to take his earlobe between her teeth, flattening her breasts against his torso. Her pebbled nipples dragged against his torso, her body on fire. She suckled on the fleshy nub of his ear before laying a fiery trail of licks and kisses down the side of his throat to nibble along the ridge of his collarbone.

Utterly fixated upon the feelings amassing inside her, she was barely aware of the bed trembling beneath their passion or the repeating *thump* of the headboard striking the wall. Neither did either of them notice the dot of crimson glowing at the base of the bedroom door.

Gnawing wantonly on his collarbone, alternating between sharp nips and soothing licks, her sounds of pleasure muffled against his shoulder as the smouldering sensations burning through her dominated her senses. She felt the fire building inside her again, preparing to erupt. God! She was close, so very close. Yet it was not enough, nowhere near enough, and unable to stand the torture a moment longer, she pushed away from the headboard. Rearing back, both hands coming round to grip his upraised knees, she tossed her head back and cried out in sheer euphoria.

"Oh, God! Mark... your dick feels so good... oh, baby-yes..." she gasped, her pert breasts bouncing in time to the rocking of her hips and tight buttocks smacking against his thighs with a lewd, wet *slap*. Using her grip on his knees to help speed her movements, she focused all her energies on reaching her peak, meeting his every thrust with a plummeting descent and grinding her pelvis against his in tight circles. Every time their bodies joined, her clit banged against his pelvic bone, igniting a lightning storm within the bundle of nerves that propelled along her spine to every fibre of her body, pushing her closer and closer to the edge of sweet oblivion. "Ugh... fuck, yes! Give it to me... I want it. Harder, oh fuck, oh fuck, fuck, fuck, fuck..."

"Ah... shit- Mina... I can-can't take it... your-your pussy is so-so... I'm going to cum!" moaned Mark, his eyes hooded and glazed, his pale skin flushed and glistening with a sheen of perspiration, and his face a mask of absolute ecstasy, contorting his features. He was bucking beneath her, his cock swelling inside and jerking excitedly as her inner walls convulsed around him, his grip on her buttocks tightening to the point of agony, both steadying her and urging her to go faster, harder.

"Yes-yes... cum inside me... grind that cock into me... fill me up- oh, my God!" Mina was frantic, rising and falling, rotating her pelvis down onto his bucking shaft's upward thrusts, riding him with such feverish abandon that her body shook as she raced towards her release. "Make my pussy cum- oh fuck- make that pussy cum again- oh God, oh God, oh God." She was so close, her clit was pulsing and she could feel a tongue of flame lash her depths, the tight knot of fire within her core rippling and quaking, sending renewed shivers of delight to prickle her skin.

Mark seemed to know just what she needed. As she writhed above him, one of his hands released its grip on her and slithered down her mound to where they were joined, and two of his fingers closed over her swollen clitoris, rolling it back and forth between the digits as though he were testing a grape. The simple touch was like a strike from a bolt of lightning. Already on sensory overload, this fresh assault pitched Mina over the edge and the plateau came upon her so abruptly she only had time to impale herself upon him, trying to take his rigid length as deep as possible, before the ball of fire erupted inside her.

It began somewhere deep inside her, a spark, a burst of white-hot fire rippling outward, coursing through her, crashing against her until it had completely overwhelmed her senses. On their own volition, her hands released their grip on his knees and rose up to tangle in her hair, her lips parting in a voiceless scream of ecstasy. The world slipped from focus as vibrant streams of aurora glazed her vision. She could feel herself shaking in throes of pleasure, every nerve in her body suddenly electrified, her muscles convulsing in a flood of liquid pleasure. Swept up in the turbulent passion of her climax, she dimly heard Mark gasp and moan, his voice low and echoing as if she were hearing him from far away, before he shuddered beneath her and a rush of molten heat flooded her depths.

When the tremors finally subsided, every muscle in her body went limp and Mina tumbled into her lover's embrace, panting long, ragged breaths as an afterglow settled over her like a warm blanket, and mini-aftershocks coursed along her nervous system. Resting her weary head just beneath his chin, she ignored the unfatigued part of her brain that insisted she should hurry this along and instead settled into a comfortable embrace, his arms encircling her narrow waist and drawing her against him as she nestled upon him, listening to his heart's erratic beating slowly settling into a rhythmic march.

She'd forgotten how much she enjoyed these moments. No words were needed. It was just the closeness, the intimacy of being with someone who knew her better than she knew herself. With Mark, there were no illusions, no promises, and she didn't have to play a character from a script or meet the public's impossible expectations. She only had to be herself, if only for these brief moments, and he would accept her for better or worse, never judging her, only loving her as only he could.

Afterglow made her eyes heavy. Snuggling into the crook of his arm, listening to the deep thumps of his steadying heartbeat, she felt the years slowly lifting until she was once again the girl crying in her room, lost and broken. It had been prom night, but she'd come home after her date had dumped her before the eyes of their entire school year. Finding the house empty, Mina had sealed herself away and wept till her eyes were red and sore and then there had been a knock on her door.

"Go away" she'd tried to yell through a fit of sobs, but her voice was little more than a croaky whisper. Mark hadn't listened and had come in. Again she demanded him to leave her alone, but he wouldn't, he'd just stood in the doorway, watching her, taking in the sight of her curled up on her bed, dress dishevelled and her makeup smeared and tear-streaked. When she finished, her little stepbrother crossed the room and swept her into his arms. Still crying, she tried to pull away and then lashed out, kicking and scratching as if she were fighting for her life before beating her hands on his chest. He never let her go. Three years younger, but already bigger and stronger, he held her close until the storm passed and she went still.

They'd remained like that for the longest time. Mina didn't say a word, only basked in the comfort of his embrace. When she did finally stir, she found him already watching her, his brown eyes big and round and glassy with fear. She'd never seen him so afraid and when their eyes met, she did the unthinkable. She kissed him. It was their first true kiss, but the first of many. In his arms, she felt free in a way she'd never thought possible. They'd tumbled together onto the bed, their lips and fingers avidly exploring this new territory. He'd set a fire in her soul and suddenly the world around them had ceased to exist. They made love well into the early hours, their hunger for each other apparently unquenchable. Though a confessed virgin, he'd played her body with an intuitive familiarity, each time building her up to new heights of pleasure before bringing her crashing down, over and over and over again, until dawn's pink and gold light had bathed their spent bodies at the peak of a final release...

Mark suddenly shifted beneath her, shattering her reverie, his softening shaft slipping from her, causing her to groan in displeasure as the feeling of emptiness that followed shattered the spell that had fallen over her, dragging her back to cold reality. She found him already watching her, his perpetually unruly hair a sweat-sodden mop of chestnut strands, falling over his eyes and a goofy smile turning the corners of his lips.

He was just so cute. The sight brought butterflies to her stomach and she leant up, pressing a gentle, almost chaste, kiss to his lips before drawing back and returning the smile. "So squirt, did you enjoy your birthday present?"

Mark's smile broadened, his eyes sparkling with emotion beneath the strands of his hair. The tip of his tongue swept across his lips, moistening them, and he brought his hand up to cup her chin, the pads of his fingertips gently brushing over the soft skin. "This was fant-"

"Well, isn't this something?"

Four

 The voice was like the crack of a bullwhip. Eyes widening, Mina whirled around toward the source, her heart leaping into her throat and a cascade of icy terror rushed over her. Standing there was none other than *little* Daniel Cornwell. His eyes were downcast and he wore a sheepish look that didn't suit his growth spurt. Fanning out on his flanks were Sean, Eric, Charlie and Victor, their lecherous stares quickly reminding her of her nudity. Her skin burned with embarrassment, so she seized a fistful of the duvet and, with a great tug, heaved the blankets up from beneath them to her chest, covering her breasts and lower body.

Oh, God, this can't be happening. How much did they see? What are we going to... no, wait, maybe they've only just arrived. Maybe we can bluff our way through this.

The door behind the boys was closed but the sounds of the party going on downstairs was as raucous as she remembered, suggesting her and Mark's absence had not been seriously noted.

"I don't know about you guys, but I'd say this party just keeps on getting better and better," sniggered Sean, his eyes gleaming with dark amusement and never once leaving the spot where her breasts had been on display just moments before.

"Hey... what the fuck, Sean! Get outta here!" Mark growled, making no effort to cover his nudity as he shot daggers at the group. Then he turned to Daniel, who shrunk slightly before his boyhood friend's betrayal. "Danny?"

"I'm sorry, man, I couldn't stop them..." Daniel, at least, had the good grace to look ashamed before giving a sideways glance towards Victor who, standing just to his left and easily the biggest of the group, must have outweighed him by more than five stone of pure muscle. Nonetheless, Mina somehow doubted the sincerity of his apology and refused to look at him. He had always been at the root of trouble.

"No, I think we'll stay," Sean declared, ignoring Daniel's hurried excuse and stepping past the pair of taller men, his toothy grin never wavering. "That was a fine show you two put on, but personally I think it deserves an encore."

What? His words sent an icy chill down her spine as dread festered in her heart. Could he possibly be suggesting what she thought he was? Were they mad? Yet when she cast her eyes over his followers, she could plainly see they were all thinking along the same lines. Did they know something she didn't? What could possibly make these brats think she'd agree to such a thing?

"What are you talking about?" snarled Mark, his voice low and deadly as he rounded back on Sean. There were only a few strides of width separating them, and Mina couldn't help but note the way Mark's fingers were twitching, as if he wanted nothing better than to strangle the weasel. It was then she noticed the gadget in Sean's hand.

"I'm talking about this." Without once taking his eyes off Mina, he raised his smartphone up for both her and Mark to see the video playing across the face. It was of poor resolution, courtesy of the extended zoom used while recording, and the sound of the party below had distorted the sound. She supposed she should have been thankful for those small mercies, but the picture was not so grainy that she could not easily recognise the rutting bodies upon the bed, seen from a dozen different angles, nor fail to identify her own pleasure-etched expression as she vigorously rode the male body beneath her. "Imagine if this went viral. Maybe I should upload it to YouTube right now? I wonder how long it would be before the media found it. Ten minutes? Five? I can just read the headlines now. *Sex Tape Released of Child Star Mina Carring Fucking Her Stepbrother.*"

Feeling suddenly numb as realisation dawned, she cast a quick glance back to his entourage to see that the trio all had their phones out, and were displaying similar recordings. "I think it's fair to say your career would be ruined. Oh, and you have a boyfriend, don't you? I wonder what he'll think of this? And your parents..."

He shrugged suggestively, and all four smiled those knowing smirks they'd worn when she saw them in the kitchen. On the outskirts of the group, Daniel's gaze darkened and he looked away. And suddenly the penny dropped.

Realisation dawned, crashing over her like a wall of icy water and leaving her feeling sick. She'd been set up. They'd known. Somehow, they had known the truth behind Mark's absence and told her where to find him so she'd walk in on him in the act, then followed her up to witness the aftermath that unfolded. No doubt they'd been hoping she would scream and shout and make a scene that would have brought the entire party crashing in, humiliating Mark on his birthday. Only it hadn't played out as expected. No, instead she'd not only played into their hands, but landed right in their pockets.

But how in God's name had they gotten in when she'd locked the door... unless.

Her eyes darted to Daniel, and it fell into place. Of course, little Danny Cornwell. A securely locked door had been no barrier to him when he was ten. Why should time, bestselling thrillers, and a military training to invade someone's privacy have done anything to deter or dissuade him?

"Why... you... son of a bitch! Give me that!" Mark roared, leaping to his feet with fists balled, about to lunge for the fiery-haired youth. Sean hastily fell back a step, clutching the device to his chest and fingers coming alive on the touchscreen. Mina seized Mark's wrist, stopping him dead.

"No, Mark," she said, her voice flat and betraying no emotion as she held him back before staring fixedly at her blackmailer. "What do you want?"

His smile broadened and Sean lowered the phone. "Hmmm... I knew you'd see things our way. What do we want? Why, we want what he had.."

"No," she growled, trying to mask her nervousness with the same cool mask of confidence she often portrayed on set. "I'll pay you whatever you want, but I'm not going to fuck you!"

"You'll do what we want. So long as we have this, we own your ass," Sean barked, his beady eyes narrowing in anger. Yet Mina held firm, her heart hammering against her chest as she tried to judge how far she could go. If they pressed her, she knew she'd have to give in, but then if they carried through with their threat, they'd get nothing. They'd have to bargain. Fortunately, Sean seemed to be thinking the same thing. "Ugh... fine! No fucking. Give us a blow job, then."

"And if I give you one, then you'll delete the videos?" she asked, her stomach roiling at the thought but managing to spit out the words. Sean nodded in confirmation. "Very well."

Mark whirled to confront her, his eyes disbelieving. "B-but Mina..."

"But what, Mark?" she snapped, rounding on him with more rancour than she intended. "What are you going to do? Beat them up and destroy their phones, hoping you can get them all in the seconds it will take for just one to upload it to YouTube?" Shrinking before the anger in her tone, Mark opened his mouth to protest, letting it hang there for a moment as he tried to find the words, then closed it in defeat.

As he sat back down on the bed, she turned back to Sean. "Just a blow job?"

"Just blow jobs," he reiterated, his smile returning and eyes twinkling with malicious excitement.

Mina nodded, her eyes boring into his with a chilly disdain, unable to look at her stepbrother for fear of what she'd see reflected in his eyes. They were bluffing. They just had to be. They must know the legal ramifications she could bring down on their heads if that video was released. At the very least it was an invasion of privacy, to say nothing of the professional and emotional damage. Yet if she called it, and they did indeed upload the video, did she dare sue and make it public record? In the court of public opinion, filing a suit was as good as announcing the video's authenticity, but to do nothing and hope the storm would blow over could be even worse. People would speculate why. And if she tried to claim the video was faked, how long would it take some pasty little techno-servant hiding in his parents' basement watching blurry Sailor Moon re-runs to download a copy and prove it was genuine?

Mina shuddered at the thought.

No, she couldn't let that video come out. If it did, the media fallout that would follow would devastate their parents, and Mark's life would be ruined, just when he was starting to come out of his shell. She might have grown out of touch with the fashions of the modern youth, but the hunt remained constant. That age-old instinct to pick out and torment an outcast. The video would paint an irresistible target on his back and render him a laughingstock for the rest of his days, and there would be nothing she could do to help him. Though they were not true blood siblings, the story would have paparazzi sniffing around and following her every move, waiting for that perfect scandal shot like hungry dogs awaiting the steak to fall from their master's plate. If just one snapped a shot of them together, it would be splashed across every trashy supermarket rag, naming them a 'real-life Cersei and Jaime Lannister.' She would never be able to see him again, never see her family again. In the end, she would have ripped her family apart, hurt everyone who ever loved her, and left nothing but a trail of pain and wreckage in her wake. She would become that which she had always dreaded. Her Mother.

Five

 "I'll do it."

Defeated, she rose up to stand upon the bed and released her grip on the sheet, a disgusted shiver running down her spine as she felt the heat of their gaze following its descent over the swells of her bosom and down the flat plane of her stomach to finally rest at the apex of her thighs. Despite his reservations, at the sight of her standing completely bare before them, even Danny could no longer hide his interest and the picture of them all ogling her nakedness so brazenly made her stomach turn.

Why don't you take a picture? It'll last longer!

Biting back the sarcastic retort, she stepped out of the pool of bedding and, stepping down from the bed, walked to the centre of the room. At her movement, Sean, Eric, Charlie and Victor seemed to awaken from their stupor and began hurriedly shedding their garments. Daniel, however, made no such move to disrobe. Despite her cool demeanour, Mina couldn't help a sense of trepidation as she watched them.

Could she really go through with this? Sex with Mark was one thing. They were more than lovers, more than siblings. He was her confidant and secret-keeper. They shared a bond that went beyond love and blood. This, however, was something else. This was blackmail, and only a judge's order away from prostitution. Could she live with herself, knowing she'd sold herself to them. What if it ever came out? She'd forever be labelled a whore. The news would destroy her father, and humiliate Jason. Her heart thundering, hot tears began to burn her eyes. She wanted to scream, to beg and plead for them not to do this, that she would pay whatever they wanted. Then she caught the icy gleam of madness in Sean's eyes, the sneer twisting his face as he kicked off his trousers, and knew it would do no good. Forcing the tears back, she took a deep, nerve steadying breath and said "Mark... please, don't look. I don't want you to see me like this."

Sinking to her knees, the carpet oddly coarse against her bare skin, she watched the naked foursome converge on her, their fully engorged arousals bobbing proudly between their legs with their movements as they fanned out, towering over her and half encircling her in a crescent ring. Despite her revulsion, Mina couldn't resist letting her eyes trail over their forms, giving them each a once-over. Sean was closest.

Neither fat nor thin, he was covered with a thin pelt of shaggy ginger curls and a nest of freckles across his abdomen. Victor stood beside him on her left, huge and broad with Herculean muscles like chiselled marble and without a trace of hair to blemish his bronzed flesh. Farthest on the right, Charlie was sword-thin with smooth, milky skin and a gold ring hanging from his right nipple. Hanging back on the left flank, stout and shaped like badly kneaded dough, Eric was by far the most comic of the group and was looking questioningly around at the others, as if waiting for instructions.

Desperate to get this over with as quickly as possible, she shuffled forward and opened her mouth. Her heart hammering against her ribs, she glanced up at Sean, saw his toothy grin and firm nod, before dipping forward. He was about average length, but his erection bent sharply upward just beneath the head and she could feel the tip of his mushroom-shaped organ scraping along the roof of her mouth as she took him into her damp cavern. Inhaling the thick musky scent of his arousal, she used the point of her tongue to lightly trace the sensitive ridges on the organ's underside while closing her lips around the place where the shaft curved and suckled lazily.

However, when he tried to grab her head, Mina slapped his hand away and pulled off. He arched a quizzical brow at her, but she held his gaze with a look of steadfast defiance. "Just a blow job. No touching."

"Oh," Sean's face softened, his eyebrow lowering, then his features hardened in a look of livid fury. He struck her with an open palm across her cheek that produced a sound like the crack of a bullwhip. "Now listen slut. I'm in charge here. Not you. Not your little fuck toy over there, or that pussy Daniel. Me!" Spittle rained from his lips as he spat the word out like a child throwing a tantrum. "So I'll touch whatever the fuck I want and if you dare say no to me again, we'll upload the videos. Got it?"

Refusing to look away, Mina touched a hand to where he'd hit her. The skin was hot against her fingers. The blow had stung, however there was little pain. It wouldn't leave a mark.

But did she dare push him further? She wasn't worried about the recordings. He couldn't upload them now. If he did, he'd lose his only leverage to get what he wanted, and he knew it. He'd threaten and shout and try to strong-arm her to his will, but it would be all bluff until he was sure she wouldn't give in. No, the videos on their phones were the least of her worries for the moment.

She cast a sidelong look at Mark upon the bed. He sat hunched over, muscles tense and fists balled amongst the sheets, ready to spring. His lips were pulled back in a deadly grimace. She could take whatever they threw at her, but he looked ready to snap at any moment. She nodded.

Sean smirked, his beady eyes glittering venomously. With the same hand that had struck her, he roughly cupped her chin and forced her eyes back to him, fingers digging into her cheeks. The touch made Mina's skin crawl yet she forced herself not to pull away and the ginger nodded too. "Good, now get back to work."

Mark shifted, and for a terrible instant, Mina was terrified he would throw himself at her abuser, but he stayed on the bed.

Loath to give this slimy weasel any pleasure, she stared up at him and forced herself to imagine her Jason standing over her, envisioning his shaggy chocolate curls and firm jaw, his broad build and crooked grin, and his deep, piercing gaze...

"Oh yeah, that's more like it... mmm- that's it, suck it, slut," moaned Sean, his head falling back in sweet euphoria as she began eagerly suckling his organ. Though the fantasy wasn't much of a distraction, it was nonetheless enough to ignite a lustful fire inside her, the flames licking that cold and empty cavern deep inside her. It fed off her every thought and grew into an all-consuming blaze that threatened to envelop her at any moment. Swept up in its roaring tide, she went to work on him, focusing all her energies on stimulating his organ's sensitised head, sucking voraciously while swirling her silky tongue around and around the slick, rubbery flesh.

As her attentions grew more impassioned, the weasel-faced Sean's breathing became laboured and his hips began to rock against her, urgently fucking her mouth's damp cavern. Adjusting to match his erratic rhythm, Mina quickened her pace, twisting her torso this way and that with such energy her perky breasts jiggled, her head rising and falling with his undulating hips, the furnace of her core growing slick with a flood of liquid desire as she imagined the familiar mask of pleasure settling over Jason's features.

Barely aware of the others arranged around her, her hands rose on their own invitation to grasp both Charlie and Eric's swollen members. As her fingers closed around them, the boys released a pair of low groans and she could feel their hard lengths writhing in her grasp. They had the feel of steel shafts wrapped in heated silk. Slurping and sucking intently on Sean's cock, being as loud and crude as possible, she began to pump her hands in perfect rhythm with the bob of her head, making all three thrust and churn into her pleasurable embrace.

"Oh, fuck... almost there, yeah... I knew you'd be a first-class cock sucker. I bet you love it, don't you... oh shit! Your mouth's so hot, I can't wait to fill it up with my cum," growled Sean, his voice hitched and the jerk of his hips growing more sporadic as a pressure gathered in the base of his spine. Mina could feel his orgasm building too. She could taste the salty flavour of his pre-cum spill across her tongue as his arousal swelled and throbbed between her lips.

The realisation was enough to break her fantasy. Sensing his desperate need to reach his peak, she felt the irresistible urge to be naughty and pulled back, pausing only to flick the weeping tip with the point of her tongue before leaving him completely. As the heat of her mouth left him, Sean visibly stiffened and turned his gaze down on her. Eyes lived and jaw clenched tight, he uttered a protesting gasp and tried to drag her back but she ducked beneath his clumsy grab.

Payback's a bitch, you little ferret-faced fucker!

Grinning inwardly, she rounded on the imposing giant standing just to her left, nearly poking her eye out as his engorged manhood jutted towards her. Despite Victor's bruiser build, his cock stood about 14 centimetres and appeared the same width as two of her slender fingers, it's bulbous crown a deep red, pulsing dangerously in testament to his arousal.

Ohhh... compensating for something are we, big boy?

Barely able to contain her amusement, and more than a little relieved to find his size was not exactly proportionate,

Mina shifted her attention from his loins and trailed a con-templating eye up his marble-like front to take in his look of intense concentration. Holding his gaze while her hands continued to work their magic upon his fellows, she bent down, her lips parting, the moist heat of her breath spilling across Victor's throbbing head.

"Ugh... I'm going to cum!" gasped Victor. It was the first time she had heard the brute speak, his voice high and uncommonly squeaky for someone of his size. Before she could absorb the hilarity of his quirks or the gravity of his statement, his engorged shaft stilled, swelled, and expelled a long rope of his creamy seed that splattered across the roof of her mouth. Surprised by his abrupt release, Mina could only stare in wide-eyed disbelief as two more bursts filled her mouth before she closed her lips and, with a shiver of disgust, swallowed the bitter fluid. Both Eric and Charlie uttered a mix of mocking laughs and pleasure-thick groans at the brute's premature climax as her hands glided along the full length of their shafts, the velvety skin slick and writhing beneath her touch, but Victor was immune to their disdain. Panting in exhaustion, his eyes closed and muscles slack, he swayed slightly before taking an unsteady step back and toppled to his arse with a force that made the floor tremble in his wake.

Sean promptly stepped over the downed behemoth, his eyes ablaze with primal hunger. Without warning, his hand seized the back of Mina's head, his fingers twisting through her hair in a grip she was powerless to resist as he dragged her forward. Overbalanced and hissing in pain, she tried to protest but before she could utter a word, the head of his cock passed between her parted lips. Eyes widening, she lurched back in sudden panic yet couldn't break his hold as he continued to apply pressure, forcing her to take him in, her lips stretching around his shaft. When her tongue brushed against his frenulum, the ginger-haired man uttered a low moan and his hips jerked, thrusting home into her warmth, causing the rubbery tip to bang against the back of her throat, triggering the terrible, jarring kick of her gag reflex. Feeling her eyes water, Mina instinctively tried to pull away, but Sean held her firm, his eyes glaring down into hers with a manic intensity as he loomed over her, daring her to make him stop.

Unable to breathe, she desperately tried to swallow his engorged organ to grab a breath, but only succeeded in making a wet, throaty gargle as her muscles drew it into her pharynx, choking her. Openly crying as his hand forcefully pressed on the back of her head, she felt his bulbous crown burrow deeper and deeper. It felt coarse, like a rolled-up sheet of sandpaper, and much larger than she remembered. Icy panic crashed over her, yet Sean was merciless and pressed on until he was fully encased within her throat, her lips nestled around his hilt and his balls banging against her chin.

Mina's jaw began to throb painfully, her head spinning from lack of oxygen. Desperate to hold on to reality, her hands stilled their movements and squeezed Eric and Charlie so tightly both boys grunted before spilling themselves into her grasp. A heavy fog of dizziness descended over her mind. Black spots danced before her eyes as her vision slipped in and out of focus and her heart thundered in her ears. Starved of oxygen and on the brink of unconsciousness, she was dimly aware of a sharp pain across her scalp as Sean's dexterous fingers fisted in her silky hair. Then he moaned something incoherent at the feel of her throat convulsing around his swollen length, released a roar of pleasure and unleashed a wash of liquid heat down her throat.

He held her there, forcing her to take in every drop off his release until his orgasm had passed and his nerveless digits released their hold. Sensing the pressure lift, she used the last of her energy to pull back, her chest heaving as his shrinking cock was removed from her airway. She dragged in great lungfuls of life-giving oxygen, only to suddenly wretch and cough violently. Doubling over as the fit inflamed her already raw pharynx, Mina had a momentary glimpse of the trio exchanging glazed looks, their manhoods shrivelled and semi-spent, before a bitter aftertaste flooded her senses and she was almost overwhelmed by the urge to vomit.

Gritting her teeth to hold off the rising tide of sickness, she brought her hands up to cover her mouth only to find her fingers doused in thick, creamy semen. Her stomach roiled as she inhaled the musky scent of the boys' climax, yet she forced herself to swallow the salty aftertaste before reaching out and picking up one of the discarded garments. Using it like a handkerchief, she towelled her hands until every last drop of their combined essence had been scrubbed from her skin. Using a clean area of the garment, Mina dabbed away her few remaining tears and wiped away any excess saliva that had spilt down her chin. Finally satisfied she was clean, but all too aware of her pressing need to take another shower before returning home, she discarded the article of clothing and turned her gaze up to see Sean, Eric and Charlie still standing over her but with their heads all turned towards the same direction and all wearing identical, knowing grins. Following their gaze back across the room, she felt her stomach plunge at the sight of Danny still standing by the door.

One more to go.

Six

 "So how bout it, Danny? Are you man enough to play with the big boys, or would you rather try your luck with Mark instead? You two always did make a cute couple," sneered Sean, his followers chuckling in agreement. They were like hyenas baiting a lion.

Daniel just stood there, his jaw tight and fists clenched. His eyes darted from one face to the next, perhaps gauging their resolve, before looking past her to where she knew Mark was watching. He held that look for a long moment, his expression shifting slightly as he and Mark exchanged a silent conversation, then his attention shifted to her and what she saw there made her stomach do cartwheels before it plummeted down a black, bottomless pit. Want. Pure, unadulterated, naked, burning, lust.

"Er... fuck you, Sean!" he growled. He then reached down, seized the hem of his black polo-top and dragged it up, revealing the hard, chiselled muscles beneath before pulling it over his head and carelessly discarding it to join the many other articles of clothing that littered the floor. Easily more Jason Statham than Arnold Schwarzenegger, Daniel's body was broad but also wiry, his pale skin stretched tight across sculpted muscles defined into works of art. The sight ignited a spark of desire inside her core and her insides lurched as he reached for the button of his dark navy jeans, a prominent bulge straining against the denim.

Crossing the room in four long strides and shouldering past his tormentors, Daniel took up a position before her, looming over her like the god Ares. Without taking his eyes off her, his fingers smoothly released the fastening of his jeans so that his engorged arousal sprang free of its confines as he pushed the garment down his thighs and knees to let them pool around his feet. Danny was left standing before her in all his Herculean glory.

Oh wow, so big. He certainly has grown up.

The dull ache in her jaw returned as she marvelled at his size, estimating him to be an easy nine inches at least. Mina gulped nervously and looked up at him with wide eyes, imploring him not to make her do this. Yet he was unmoved, his normally pale and impish blue eyes dark and smouldering with desire as he drank in the sight of her naked body kneeling before him. Crestfallen, but nonetheless determined not to let him see her sweat, she rose back up to her knees and, refusing to meet his gaze, obediently parted her lips.

"No."

Mina stilled, more out of surprise than obedience, not daring to believe her own ears but hoping against hope her prayers had been answered and she would not be forced to endure this last, humiliating disgrace. Yet the feeling of his powerful hand coming to rest comfortingly on her shoulder made her heart leap all the same and slowly, cautiously, she tipped her head back. She only caught a glimpse of his bright, toothy grin before his hand suddenly pushed her backward. Caught off guard, she gasped in surprise and twisted with his hand to tumble to the ground in a heap on her front with her backside raised in the air, her landing blessedly cushioned by the carpet beneath.

"Danny? Wha-?" Her voice failed her as, looking back over her shoulder, stray strands of her golden hair falling over her eyes, she glimpsed him step out of his pooled jeans and sink to his knees behind her, his erection jutting out before him.

The sight sent an icy cascade down her back and, realising his intention, she wheeled in desperate flight and began to crawl away only to have his hands snap out and seize her narrow waist in a vice-like grip that held her firm. Her heart pounded in renewed panic as she began to claw at the carpet, desperate to get away. Yet, against Daniel's awesome strength, she may as well have been wearing knitted mittens and he effortlessly dragged her back. "No! No! Let go of me! We had a deal. I said I'd only give you a blow job, nothing more. You can't do this!" she pleaded, yet despite her protests she couldn't help a low sigh when his tapered tip brushed against her still engorged clitoris.

Her stomach tightening into tight knots, she cast a desperate look around the room, hoping against hope that perhaps Sean or one of his followers might step in to stop this but, to her horror, they were all making themselves comfortable on the sofa, wearing wide grins and hooting encouragement. Even Mark was as quiet as a mouse and couldn't meet her gaze as his renewed erection stood to attention between his thighs. For all his objections, he seemed to have quite enjoyed the show.

Treacherous littleshit!

"Yes, well, I never agreed to that deal," Daniel growled, his voice thick and guttural with primal passion as a toothy grin transformed his handsome features into a predatory mask. "Besides, I've waited too long to have you like this to just let this chance pass me by!" He snapped his hips forward.

"No!" she cried, but her protests dissolved into a pleasured moan as she felt her swollen folds part beneath his blunt tip, the rounded head pushing effortlessly through the tight ring of muscle into the cavern beyond. Mouth ajar and eyes widening, Mina wanted to scream, yet, unable to speak through the feeling of him entering her, she could only whimper and gasp. Danny drove on regardless however, his fingers tightening to a near bruising intensity, drawing her back as he edged forward, pushing deeper into her snug warmth.

No! Stop! You're going to rip my pussy apart!

He was so big. It felt as if he were splitting her in two and she could feel the shaft's every vein and ridge rub against her inner walls as he pierced her core, stretching the plush, yielding flesh and tight ring of muscle to its limit as she struggled to accommodate his impressive girth. Deep down she knew she should not be enjoying this, that it was wrong, that he was as good as raping her, but her body was betraying her and she could feel herself growing wet with desire. Torn between burning agony and exquisite ecstasy, repulsion and delight, she clutched the carpet in white-knuckled fists and took everything he had to give, her back curling at the feeling of sheer fullness, until he was fully sheathed within her tight embrace, his hard pelvis nestled against the full curves of her upturned buttocks.

"Oh wow... th-this is great," Daniel grunted, his arousal nestled so deep within her he was very nearly at the mouth of her womb. Then, without giving her time to adjust, he began to pull out, leaving a cold and terrible emptiness in his wake. Exhaling a relieved sigh, Mina used the momentary reprieve to catch her breath, yet despite her best efforts to appear unaffected, her walls clung to him, attempting to draw him back. When only the bulbous crown was lodged within the gates of her dew-slickened womanhood, she couldn't help dread the impending loss. Just before he slipped from her snug embrace, he drove back inside her hard and fast, making the beauty gasp involuntarily in a delicious cocktail of pain and pleasure as his heavy shaft plunged deeper, the sensation overbalancing her senses and setting off a burst of starlight behind her eyes. Yet it was only the beginning. Taking her gasp as a signal to continue, Daniel began to snap his hips back and forth, establishing a fast, feral rhythm, his strokes deep and hard and growing more wild with his every re-entry until he was savagely pounding her up-thrust womanhood with primeval ardour. "So-so tight... it- it's even better than I imagined."

"You- you mean you've imagined this? You've thought about fucking me before?" gasped Mina, breathless, overwhelmed, and utterly lost in the sensation of his big, hard cock pillaging her depths, yet all the while trying desperately to keep her senses. With his every thrust, a surge of raw sensation crashed over her as he created such sweet friction inside her, the pain of his initial entry long forgotten, making her head spin and body throb with white-hot pleasure.

Daniel grunted in affirmation, driving into her so forcefully she couldn't restrain the small groans of pleasure that escaped her lips. "W-when I was younger. I couldn't help it... you're just so gorgeous! I-I'd get so hard every time I saw you, and I lost count of how many times I masturbated while thinking about you. Sometimes, when I was spending the night round, I would even pretend to be asleep and when I heard you go for a shower, would sneak out, force the bathroom door open a crack, and spy on you..."

The beauty moaned at his confession. "Oh- fuck... you were always such a bad boy. Did watching me make your big dick hard? Did you enjoy seeing me all wet and soapy? Did it get you hot, being a dirty peeping Tom, imagining what my body felt like, what I'd do to you if I caught you?" Mina couldn't believe what she was saying. The very idea that Daniel had been spying on her made her clitoris throb. It was still hard for her to believe this was really happening. She was actually being fucked by her stepbrother's best friend and, deep down, she was allowing it to happen.

God, this is crazy, what am I doing? Why am I not stopping him?

It would be so easy, all it would take was one word from her, a scream, a shout, just one little command and he would cease the maddening assault that was making her blood simmer.

Yet it feels so good!

She was shaking, her mind reeling, revelling in the speed and forcefulness of his deep, pummelling strokes, the feeling of his thick cock rocking within her, fucking her, stretching her, filling her like none ever had before, making her feel like an innocent virgin, and powerless to silence the moans spilling from her in hot, lustful pants. Every time he drove into her, she could feel him rub against her inner walls, and as he pulled out, the swollen ridge of his corona dragged against their tight embrace, sending fiery bursts of pleasure surging up her spine. She'd had several lovers over the course of her life, but this was the first time one had ever used her like this. Never before had she been fucked so forcefully, so deeply, so purposefully. It felt like she was going to burst in the most wondrous way and as her knees began to grow hot, she anticipated having some very difficult-to-explain rug burns in the morning.

"Yeah, and whenever I caught you mas-masturbating with the shower head... Oh fuck..." Daniel's voice trailed off for a moment, as if he were trying to relive the treasured memory, and his fierce pace wavered slightly as he tried to breathe, speak, and moan all at once. "It got me so fucking horny. I couldn't help reaching into my boxers and imagine I was fucking you against the glass."

Mina couldn't stand it any longer.

Oh God... Mark, forgive me but I can't take any more.

"Then... mmm... what are you waiting for...fuck me! Fuck me with that big cock... I want it!" she begged, surrendering to the fiery storm of pleasure raging inside her core.

Biting her lower lip in sinful ecstasy, she shot him a wanton look back over her shoulder and watched his handsome features grow tight with pleasure as her hands pushed against the carpet to meet his strokes, her full buttocks meeting his hard abdomen with a wet *slap*. Rocking to the rhythm of his thrusts, drawing herself forward as he withdrew only to slam backward to take him as deep as possible on re-entry, she fucked him back with equal vigour, a low moan rising in the back of her throat as she felt his length tunnel deeper into her warmth. He felt so big. It was a wonder her body could take all of him in.

"Mmm... your cock's so big and hard! Oh-yes- pull me back on that dick...make me take it, I want it, I want it!" she heard herself pleading, the words spilling from her in a lustful tide as liquid pleasure pulsed through her veins. Mina rocked urgently against Daniel's thrusts, bouncing and grinding her shapely rear upon his driving cock while she tossed her head from side to side in maddening delirium. She could feel herself tighten as she approached her third climax of the evening, an infernal storm of molten sensations gathering deep within her with each stroke.

It would not be long now. Already she was approaching the summit, hanging on the brink of that sweet abyss as his magnificent cock stretched her almost to the point of breaking. Yet it was not enough. Needing more, she released her right hand's death grip and blindly reached beneath her.

Cupping his swinging testicles in her palm, she could just hear his ragged breaths and low groans every time he drove into her as she groped the velvety sack, her index finger gently prodding his rocking perineum, his low, guttural sounds of pleasure driving her wild until she couldn't stand it any longer. Relinquishing her grip on him, her searching fingers slid up to nestle between her gyrating thighs and attack her swollen clit, urgently seeking the release her body so desperately craved.

"Mm- mmmm- oh God! Oh fuck! Oh!" she gasped, her cries arching in sensual delight, her movements becoming almost frantic as she expertly manipulated the bundle of nerves. Rolling her fingers counter clockwise, her legs began to tremble and shake as hot pulses surged through her nervous system, heightening the sensation of his thick cock filling her. "Ohh... oh! I can't take it... it's too good... don't stop. Fuck me! Fuck me! I'm cumming! I'm cumming!" Then her orgasm hit her.

It began with a slight tremor in her lower abdomen that spiralled along her nerves to her nipples, radiating throughout her body in intense waves as the burning heat within her erupted. Overwhelmed, flashes of colour ignited behind her eyelids and her head snapped back, a voiceless cry spilling from her parted lips as every muscle in her body shook and the hand that had been vigorously rubbing her clit abandoned its ministrations to rise up and fist in her silken locks. She felt like she was burning in a fire of pure sexual passion and she vaguely registered Daniel's strained groan as she writhed around him, yet he never let up and continued pounding her with deep lunging strokes, fucking her through one release and into another.

"Holy... fuck, fuck, fuck, fuck! Oh God. Oh... Oh, fucking God I can't stop cumming!" wailed Mina, thrashing uncontrollably as an even stronger climax suddenly overtook her, plunging the euphoric beauty into the fires of sensory oblivion.

So- so hot, oh God! It's too fucking incredible! I can't stand it!

Moaning and gasping with every breath, her only thought was to escape this sex god's clutches before he killed her and she desperately tried to stand, only her legs were shaking uncontrollably as wave after white-capped wave crashed over her and they could not support her.

Taking advantage of her helplessness, Daniel drew back and then plunged into her to the hilt, fully sheathing himself within her before going still as his hands relaxed their hold on her hips and slid down her quaking legs to seize her ankles. With a predatory growl, he jerked them back, causing his lover to gasp in alarm as he bent the limbs back until her feet were pressing against her buttocks, spreading her open, before clambering to his feet and adjusting his grip to hook his fingers over her hips while pressing his wrists against her heels to pin them in place.

Upside-down and hanging near vertical from his arms, Mina couldn't help mewing uncontrollably as Daniel resumed wildly fucking her upraised sex, his powerful hands easily supporting her suspended hindquarters. He was like a machine, never wavering, driving into her heat with long, deep strokes and as he established a merciless rhythm, the bedroom seemed to come alive with the whoops and cheers of their audience. Strangely, the sounds of their applause did little to impede her burning desire. Consumed by the primitive pleasure of being dominated, the beauty had forgotten that she and Daniel were far from alone in the room, but now the idea that her tormentors, not to mention Mark, were watching her in this shameful position, being fucked by this young stud with a big cock, made her clit and pussy throb.

"Oh fuck! You-you dirty bastard, you're going to make me cum again! Oh my God... oh... oh... oh yes" she hissed, "take that pussy... make me take all that dick... I love it... I love it!" In this position, she was completely open and vulnerable to her lover's every desire. Pure carnal heat spread through her abdomen, signalling that her next climax was already building. Mina desperately tried to match his pace, but he was thrusting into her so forcefully it drove all thoughts from her mind, leaving her basking in a hazy fog. She could feel his arousal's mushroom-shaped head penetrate her depths, stretching her plush core as his hips continued to snap back and forth, filling her completely with each hard stroke. Mina struggled not to scream as each lunging thrust jolted her body, hitting her sweet spot every time, sending hot surges of near orgasmic sensation rushing through her.

"Fuck! Yeah... is this what you want? You want my big cock fucking your tiny pussy? Then cum, cum, cum..." grunted Daniel, his tone guttural and breathing laboured. He must have been close, for Mina could sense the pressure gathering within him behind his motions, but he was stubbornly trying to hold it at bay while doubling his efforts, fucking her with the single-mindedness of a rutting beast, seemingly determined to ensure she reached her peak first. For Mina, it was all too much.

Delighting in the sensation of him slam into her scorching depths, the enraptured actress could do little more than mew, gasp, and moan, wide-eyed as her arms gave way beneath the onslaught. Supported only by his tight grip, his increasing vigour fed the fires spreading through her core and sent her spiralling towards completion. Crumpling into the carpet's soft embrace with arms outstretched, her succulent rump held up only by Danny's powerful hands, she buried her face into the floor to muffle her cries while her pebbled nipples temptingly rubbed against the textile. Her toes curled and her spine arched as he hammered away at her unforgivingly, driving her down into the carpet. His thick length surged harder and deeper into her tight sheath, sending intense surges of pleasure crashing over her and driving her closer and closer to the brink. A Herculean thrust penetrated all the way to her cervix and the cocktail of agony and ecstasy pushed her over the edge.

She began to shiver, the orgasm sweeping through her like a tsunami as the burning ball deep in her core erupted and great quaking tremors of release rippled outward to tingle in the tips of her fingers and pebbled nipples. Consumed by its irrepressible storm, her senses exploded as streams of light and colour danced behind her eyes once more. Rolling her head back, eyes wide and lips parted in a silent scream, she desperately clawed the carpet, seeking some sort of purchase against her spiral, before she lost herself, her nerves afire with carnal energy.

"Ah! Ah I'm cumming! Ah, oh my God... ah, ah-I'm cumming... cumming... cummming..." Regaining her voice, Mina suddenly knew she was screaming but no longer cared who heard her and gleefully gave voice to her pleasure, certain her cries could be heard amidst the blaring party below. It was as if her world was being swallowed by the unquenchable fire raging between her thighs. So intense were the feelings coursing through her and eyes rolling, she rocked, shook, and thrashed, euphoria smashing against her.

His stamina was truly amazing. Even as she quaked, erratic convulsions gripping his thick, thrusting cock, he was keeping up a constant pace, driving into her relentlessly, pushing her pleasure on and on until his every thrust was bringing her to orgasm.

Oh... God, when did I become so orgasmic?

"Ugh... I'm going to cum!" The words came shuddering from Danny in a low growl, cutting through her cries as her writhing walls rippled and clenched around him, trying to hold him deep inside her, her nectar dousing his swollen shaft before flowing freely down her abdomen. At his words and desperate tone, Mina felt another climax pulse through her and threw a look back over her shoulder, greedily admiring the sight of his pale skin glistening with a sheen of sweat, eyes shut and brow furrowed with concentration. His square jaw was tight and his muscles bulged as he struggled to hold back his release. Yet, even when racing towards his own fiery oblivion, he didn't pause, but switched to curling his hips against her upraised buttocks, urgently grinding his manhood into her sensitised pussy as his grip tightened, nails biting almost painfully into the silken flesh of her inner-thighs.

"Oh, oh fuck... mmmm you dirty boy, please... cum for me, cum in my mouth," she purred, her lips curling with a seductive smirk as she drank in the sight of her lover through glazed eyes, suddenly overwhelmed by the need to taste him. "Oh yes. I want it, let me suck you, I want to taste my pussy on your big fucking cock as I suck you dry..."

Grunting with pleasure, Daniel gave a quick nod of affirmation before cautiously edging back, withdrawing from her quivering folds and carefully lowered her lower half to the floor. Her befuddled mind barely registered the tingling numbness in her knees as his weight left her, Mina shakily pushed up from the carpet and pivoted around to find him looming over her, his rigid manhood, flushed deep crimson and roped from root to head with swollen veins, almost poked her eye out as it urgently awaited her attentions.

Licking her lips at the sight, her heart pounded excitedly with the thought of drinking his thick, creamy seed. She cocked her head and traced her eyes up his torso, considering the splendour of his lightly-toned abs and his pectorals that gleamed with a light sheen of sweat, to meet his lust-fogged orbs.

"Mmm... cum for me, baby," Mina purred, holding his gaze while she flashed him a sultry smirk, swooping down and hungrily taking just the pulsing head between her lips.

Closing her lips around the silky skin just beneath his corona, she suckled fiercely, practically raping him with her mouth, moaning at the heady cocktail of their combined flavours, as well as from the way her sex was convulsing to the echoing memory of his presence inside her, making her feel like he was still fucking her.

"Oh... fuck!" Daniel groaned in a tone low and strained, his head rolling back at the heavenly feeling of her mouth enveloping him. His hands came up to hold the sides of her head, his fingers lacing through the damp, silken strands of her hair.

Though not forcing her to take him any deeper, he had a firm hold on her to keep her in place. Mina watched him intently through sly eyes, smirking inwardly at the display of pleasure she had drawn from him, Mina curled her tongue around his sensitised tip, swirling it around and around. As her mouth worked her wonders, she brought her hands up, gently cupping the weight of his velvety sack in one while the other wrapped around his shaft, barely able to close her fingers around him, stroking the base in time with the motions of her tongue as she licked, sucked, and moaned.

"Ugh... Mi-Mina.. I'm... I'm..." Daniel gasped, knees quaking and his voice hoarse and urgent. Feeling his fingers tense in her hair, signalling his imminent release, Mina refused to relent and sucked enthusiastically, watching him squeeze his eyes shut before he emitted a low groan. A stream of thick, creamy seed erupted into her waiting orifice, splashing the back of her throat. Moaning happily, she greedily swallowed every drop as three more bursts of the salty elixir flooded her mouth. Though she had never really been a fan of swallowing, mostly out of fear of her pesky gag reflex, there was something about the taste of him that she found so addictive and it was only when she had drunk down all of his cum and his erection was beginning to soften did she release his shaft.

"Mmm... delicious," she purred, licking all traces of his release from her lips and watching the tension flood from her lover as he opened his eyes and blink repeatedly through a surge of dizziness as his senses returned. Yet before he could say anything in response, a hand suddenly seized Mina's shoulder and snatched her back, casting her to the floor. Landing on her back, she shook off her initial shock and looked up to find Sean kneeling over her, his crooked erection standing rampant between knobbly legs covered in a pelt of wiry ginger curls, the curved head swollen and glistening with pre-cum.

"Hmm- my turn!" he said, a snide sneer playing across his weasel face. Panting with desire and still trembling with the aftershocks of so many simultaneous orgasms, she watched through hazy eyes as he spread her legs apart and shuffled forward, moving into position, and in her pleasure-drunk state she never thought to protest. With a single hard thrust, he plunged into the pulsing liquid heat of her canal.

Though he was easily the smallest of her lovers, in all regards, Mina couldn't help but gasp with delight at her own violation as she felt her well-sodden womanhood take him in to his base, responding to his presence by tightening around the turgid shaft, and delectable pleasure surged through her once more.

Emitting a low groan at the sensation of her plush walls caressing his engorged flesh, Sean didn't waste a moment and, bracing his arms just above her shoulders, looming over her like a lecherous fiend of myth, began to grind into her, his hips rocking as he drew back before lunging forward like a barbarian, fucking her.

His pace was uneven but fast and rough, and he employed a rhythm of erratic stabbing thrusts meant only to heighten his own pleasure, a self-serving kind often learnt from frequent masturbation and watching too much porn, that had his features twisting. Mewing at the intoxicating sensation of the shaft's hooked head rubbing against the roof of her sheath, stimulating the sweet spot beneath her clitoris, Mina didn't resist and wound her arms around his neck as her lithe form arched, hugging his thighs with her knees, mild but undeniable pleasure spiralling through her core.

"Oh yeah! You like it, don't you, whore," Sean growled breathlessly, his misshapen manhood punching into her warm silken depths and balls slapping against her arse, the primitive pace growing more erratic as his pleasure built and perspiration dotted his skin. "Fuck... your pussy's so wet, you fucking slut. You want our silence? Then buy it. Buy it. Fuck that dick, take it all the way in your wet greedy cunt! I bet this is the best fuck of your life, go on, scream how great this is, how my big dick is the best you've ever had!"

Trying to tune out the sound of Sean's voice, Mina wanted to deny his bombastic accusation, yet her body was nonetheless responding to his mocking, trying to draw what pleasure she could from the fucking by raising her hips to meet his crude lunges. He barely filled the chilly void Daniel's absence had left inside her, but her head rolled back and little moans flowed from her parted lips while her nails hooked into this loathsome male's shoulders, making him hiss with pain.

No, she had to stop. This wasn't who she was. She didn't want this. She didn't do things like this, didn't enjoy things like this. This was so very wrong. It made her feel dirty and bad and... hot.

With his head dipped, his thin lips claimed hers, forcing her mouth open and muffling her moans as his slimy tongue thrust across her tongue. She could taste the sour cocktail of alcohol and dehydration on his breath, yet despite her revulsion, she kissed back with equal gusto, tongues battling and teeth gnashing. Keeping up his brutal assault on her delicate womanhood, Sean held the lip lock until her oxygen-starved lungs began to burn. As he finally drew back, she snatched a quick breath before leaning up, catching his lower lip between her teeth and gnawing it savagely. Yelping in alarm, Sean's hips suddenly bucked beneath, grinding deliciously against her bundle of nerves and making her gasp with delight as sparks of sweet pleasure burst behind her eyes.

Using her momentary distraction to escape, the fiery-haired delinquent moved downward, nipping a trail of fire down her milky flesh to the perky mounds of her breasts, the moist heat of his breath causing her skin to rise with goose bumps. He captured a coral pink nipple between his teeth and gnawed it like a piece of gristle. Feeling the sting of sharp-edged incisors tug her sensitised nub, her skin crawled but her desire grew and Mina began to squirm and writhe against his crude thrusts in search of greater pleasure. The rough treatment was enough to keep her on edge, making her nipples ache and her abused pussy yearn for attention, yet it remained far from adequate, keeping her only on the brink.

As he worked to get himself off, Sean didn't notice the titanic figure come up behind him until a squeaky voice said, "Hey Sean, I want to fuck her too."

The announcement made the ginger go suddenly still. Slowly releasing her brutalised breast, his breathing rasping and his lust-fogged eyes narrowed, he shot a look back across his shoulder. Following his gaze, Mina found the imposing form of Victor standing over them, his hairless body stripped naked with a renewed erection barely visible between marble-chiselled thighs. Even in her deranged state, the sight was almost comical.

"Wait your turn, *quick draw,*" hissed Sean, a snide sneer twisting his lips as he laid another hard thrust into Mina to show his disdain.

"But I want to fuck her now!" Even in such an unnaturally high and squeaky voice, the unspoken threat was as clear and as deadly as a bare length of cold, naked steel and made all the clearer by the golem's terrible look of determination. Sean's confidence evaporated beneath Victor's stern expression. His smile faltered and he glanced nervously between the lustful beauty lying beneath him and the muscular goon.

Mina was his prize. Sean had wanted her the very moment she had slinked past them in the doorway without a backwards glance, like they were beneath her. Well, now she was beneath him. He'd stolen her, made her get on her knees, and beg for his cock like the whore she was. Why should he share his toy with this thick headed brute?

But then, Victor was the only thing protecting him from Daniel and Mark's terrible vengeance.

He was torn. Caught between a not so metaphorical rock and this soft lush place, but no more willing to give up his prize than he was willing to risk pissing off Victor and getting his ass kicked by her lovers-

His smirk returned, flashing a glimpse of predatory teeth and Mina felt her stomach roil with a forbidding sense of dread as his eyes settled upon her.

"Very well..." With a sudden burst of strength, Sean lurched sideways, rolling them over, causing her to gasp with alarm as her body was dragged with him and their positions switched. Finding herself sitting upright, she could only look dazedly between the pair, her world spinning until she felt hands curl around her hips and cool fingers hook between her buttocks, spreading her open and sending a foreign shiver racing up her spine. "Fuck her here."

And the reality of her situation came crashing down as a cold wash cascading down her back.

"What! You're- you're joking, right? No! No you can't! I don't want- I've never- no!" she cried, trying to break free by thrashing violently and pushing away from Sean's body, but the male's grip was too strong and her current position meant her every motion caused the cock inside her to lurch. Her sensitised clitoris ground against his pelvis, sending reluctant pleasure shooting along her nervous system, weakening her resolve. Heart thundering, she threw a desperate look back over her shoulder at Victor, hoping against hope the brute might be repulsed by the suggestion of fucking her arse, but to her dismay his face seemed to light up at the prospect.

"Really? Cool!" In his jubilation, his voice sounded more like a giant mouse's squeak than a voice, and in any other circumstance Mina would have found it a comical spectacle, but her thoughts were too consumed with dread. With bated breath, she watched the titan sinking to his knees behind her. Then unable to watch anymore, she looked away, starring doggedly ahead, refusing to look at either of them. Just the thought of seeing Sean's cocky weasel smirk and pale eyes gleam victoriously was more than she could stand.

Hands seized her waist, huge and as rough as sandpaper against her softer skin, holding her steady as an immense bulk bore down on her from behind, pressing her farther down upon the shaft spearing her pussy. Then she felt it, the blunt, moistened tip of the brute's cock, clumsily prodding the cleft of her buttocks. Three times he missed, and she couldn't help but gasp as each jab bumped against her tailbone or her tender unaccustomed skin. When he hit his mark, she sensed a terrible pressure push against her anus, the tight little ring of muscle tightening on reflex, trying to keep the invading mass out. Regardless, Victor pushed on, forcing his cock's tapered head through her sphincter into the dry heat of her virgin arse.

Eyes watering and palms braced against Sean's chest, her nails bit into his flesh and her breath hissed through clenched teeth. Mina wanted to scream as she felt her body open, stretching to accommodate the hard length. Sharp, stinging pain burned outwards from her abused hole as the giant drove into her without mercy. She knew she needed to relax or the pain would only grow worse, but her muscles had tensed involuntarily and even Victor's diminutive shaft felt suddenly huge.

"Ohh- fuck- yeah... she likes it, Victor. When you put your dick in her ass, this slut's pussy got so tight I almost fucking blew a load. I- fuck- bet she can't wait to get double barrelled..." moaned Sean, biding his time and remaining still beneath her, basking in the feeling of her inner walls clench around him as Victor forced her toned derriere to take him all in.

"It's fucking incredible!" squeaked Victor, squeezing his eyes shut as he buried the last inch of his dick in her rectum, almost losing himself in her rear passage's exquisite tightness. Saved only by the lingering desensitisation brought about by his last orgasm, he didn't waste a moment and slowly dragged his length halfway out before driving back in, working his hips back and forth, sawing in and out of her bum, growling and panting like a wild beast.

Pinned between the two hard bodies, Mina had no choice but to weather the storm as unadulterated shame burned a hole in her soul and foreign, but not entirely unfamiliar, sensations savaged her body. Her arse was blazing yet no matter how much she wanted to ease the burning agony, to reach back and stop the burly bruiser, her body wouldn't respond to her commands. Her tense muscles froze, and no words would form, so she was forced to endure the unweathering barrage. Then slowly, with fatigue and exhaustion beginning to take their heavy toll, her tired muscles began to relax and the fiery torment ravaging her anus melted away to leave a feeling of numbness before blooming into a feeling of deep tingling pleasure. It was far from jaw-dropping, but she could sense the pressure moving through her and, to her eternal disgust and self-loathing, she began to pant with elation at the sensation of each stroke getting faster and harder as Victor's entrances became easier, until the brute was fucking her full force.

Then, sensing the change stirring within her, with a gay whoop, Sean began to move beneath her, his hips bucking and his crooked cock stabbing her depths, sending a shiver of abject pleasure rippling through her. Her body responded instinctively, a flurry of gasps and short moans escaping her throat at the feeling of their hard lengths driving into her, sending her soaring into a sexual haze.

N-no... this can't be happening!

"What a dirty fucking slut. You like it, don't you? Both your holes are twitching. I bet you just love taking two cocks at once like some back-alley whore. Yeah, that's right... take them... take them, you horny fucking slut!" grunted Sean, emphasising each guttural slur with a sharp upwards thrust that rubbed along the slick roof of her grasping sheath and sent mini shocks pulsing through her core.

"Fu-fuck you... you bastards... no... no... not so hard!" she muttered, gnawing her bottom lip between her teeth to keep from uttering any further hints of desire as the pair began to fuck her in unison, her body rocking as they used both her nether holes for their pleasures. It was random and chaotic, with both men competing in a race to reach their gratification first, without a thought for a rhythm or coordination. One instant, they would drive into her as one, making her skin feel suddenly too tight and heart thunder, then Victor would draw out suddenly whilst Sean was still languishing in her muggy embrace and they would slide in and out of her successively, speeds varying until once again they would slam into her at once. It was dark and primitive and with none of the fluidity she needed to ride to release, just a barbaric hunger that constantly pummelled her fragile being, repeatedly dragging her towards a wretched peak only to suddenly cast her down.

Mina had never felt so ashamed. To know this was happening, and worse, that she was allowing it to happen, betraying everyone she held dear, made her feel like such a slut. Desperate to distract herself from the perverted reality of her situation, she glimpsed movement out of the corner of her eye and pivoted to see a naked Daniel moving around the mass of bodies to sit beside the equally naked Mark on the bed. They sat straight-backed, rigged and tense, a difficult silence hanging over them, their eyes darting around the room, not looking at each other but careful to avoid any glance towards the spectacle taking place before them in the centre of the room. Daniel took a breath, opened his mouth as if to speak, held it there, then shut it again, the do or die-first into the breach- momentum dying away as the weight of the night's events suddenly bore down on them.

It was finally Mark who broke the stalemate. Though their exchange appeared heated, in her current state Mina hadn't a hope of hearing what was being said over the barrage of grunts and moans filling her ears. She could only hope their friendship survived this ordeal.

A slender body moved round from her opposite side to stand in front of her, blocking her view of Mark and Daniel and presenting her with a very erect, cut penis. Confronted by the sudden vision of masculinity staring her in the eye, she glanced up, drinking in the gracefully willow frame and pale ivory skin, to find Charlie's stubble-roughened face gazing placidly back down at her. Though he didn't say a word, his meaning was plain. Knowing what he wanted, she saw little point in resisting. Opening her lips, she bent forward, taking his neglected phallus, its glistening crown, and its velvety length into her mouth. At the feeling of her soft lips as they wrapped around his sensitive manhood, Charlie gasped in sweet wonderment and his hands came up to fist in her dishevelled mass of yellow tresses. She began sucking him off while Sean and Victor continued pummelling her mercilessly from behind and below.

"Hey! Wait... guys... that's not fair! I don't want her hand again. I've already had a hand job! Now I want to fuck her too!" bawled Eric in a whining, childish tone, causing Mina to glance to her right where she could just make him out, standing on the edge of her vision, small and round and unashamedly stroking his renewed erection as he watched the scene unfold with unshed tears shining in his eyes. He made a pathetic spectacle, like a spoilt, fully-grown toddler crying for another bag of sweets.

"Ugh... Don't be su-such a baby, Eric... Does it look like she has another hole for you to fuck? And I'm not about to share this tight pussy-fuck! Her pussy's getting so wet from sucking Eric off, oh... yeah, that's it! Squeeze my dick dry, slut- so shut up and just enjoy whatever you get," snapped Sean, panting with pleasure as he drove into her at an ever more erratic pace, drawing closer and closer to his second release of the night. "You-you're so pathetic, you should consider yourself the luckiest motherfucker on earth we even let you join in."

"But Sean..."

"It's alright Sean," interrupted Victor. "You remember that girl I dated last year, Miranda? She had a thing for anal and would often stick her dildo up my arse while we were fucking, sometimes she would even fuck me with a strap-on she kept under her bed, so if the fat little piggy's really that desperate he can-"

The veil lifted in the blink of an eye and Eric looked suddenly appalled by the suggestion. "What! Fuck no! I'm not gay, Victor, you faggot!"

"Fuck you, Eric! You're only gay if you're attracted to men and want to suck cock," snapped the brute, his absurdly high voice rising even higher in his fury, and his skin, stretched tight over rippling muscles, flushed to the colour of a baby tomato. "An ass is just another hole to fuck, and as I'm the one who'll be getting fucked, either come over here and stick your dick in me, or just go jerk off. I don't really care which."

Cowed by the naked fury in the larger man's voice, Eric looked down at his feet and shuffled awkwardly from foot to foot before moving around outside of Mina's line of sight. She shifted to follow but Charlie's grip on her hair held her steady and so, desperate to distract herself from the storm ravaging her lower body, she gave up and focused all her attention on worshiping his cock. Sucking furiously and bobbing her head, she slid back along his length before swooping down, taking him deeper on every swing until his fleshy cap banged against the back of her throat. She could only moan at the musky flavour spilling over her tongue, her

throat relaxed and the agony of her gag reflex remaining
a distant memory. Groaning, Charlie quickly began to roll
his hips with her motions, trying to receive more of the
wondrous sensation as his iron-hold in her hair forced her
to take him deeper and faster. And for a brief time the trick
seemed to work. Focused as she was on the job-in-mouth, she
felt detached, almost disembodied, from the foreign forces
moving within her.

Then something new off-balanced her. First, she felt Victor shudder and release a long, low breath that tickled the
hairs along the back of her neck. Then he doubled over,
burying his face in the crook of her shoulder as the cock in
her arse seemed to become even harder, and she knew Eric
had taken him up on his offer.

It was awkward, at first, but after a moment the pair fell
into rhythm and Mina could feel the doughy male's thrusts
into the brute's tight cheeks as a drumming echo that rippled
through the layers of muscle to reverberate through her anus
as Victor drove into her at the same instant. In the back of
her mind, Mina couldn't help but envision the scene unfold-
ing behind her. Victor, so huge and powerful, with bronzed
skin stretched tight over bulging muscles and glistening
with perspiration, doubled over with his features locked in a
mask of pleasure as Eric, red-faced and panting, drove into
his arse. Despite his objections, he was taking to the anal
dalliance like a natural, eagerly venting his frustration out on
the larger male's arsehole and fucking him with ill-disguised
delight, his fleshy body jiggling with each fresh plunge. The
thought sent a kinky thrill straight down to her core.

Oh... God no! Wh-why is this turning me on?

Sucking with a mad fury, she worked the cock in her mouth with all the fever of a professional as Charlie clutched at her head with both hands and began to buck and thrust into her moist orifice, trying to distract herself once more from the liquid desire surging through her veins, igniting an all-too-familiar fire in her core. Yet it did no good. The room was heavy with the scent of sex. Every breath flooded her lungs with the musky aroma of sweaty man-flesh, causing a fog to fall over her thoughts as her ears rang with the repeated slapping of flesh on flesh and the deep throaty sobs and moans of pleasure.

Her clit, swollen and in desperate need of proper attention, was throbbing. Her nipples were painfully tight, aching for devotion, and before she realised what she was doing, one of her hands relinquished their perch on Sean's torso to creep up her toned abdomen and cup the swell of her left breast, kneading it the way only she knew how while twisting the pebbled nipple between her thumb and forefinger. Just that simple touch was enough to send tingling feelings surging down to her neglected clit and she couldn't resist moaning around the dick in her mouth. Unaccustomed to being so helpless, she longed to grab them as her hips began to roll and push against the shafts hammering her twitching holes, riding them and pivoting in just the right angle to quicken the heat amassing slowly within her while the press of bodies kept her restrained, bound like a rag doll.

No-no I can't cum from this… not like this…

Then, just as the fires began to creep from her core, fingers of molten passion, the vision of her masturbating became too much for her oppressors and she suddenly felt Sean stiffen beneath her.

"Oh yeah! Here I fucking cum!" he roared, his hips bucking off the carpet in two last upward thrusts before his length suddenly swelled and erupted within her, unleashing thick streams of his molten seed deep into her grasping sheath.

Mina wanted to protest, to shout that she wasn't ready, but sensing the heat blossoming deep within her, mixing with the cum already deposited in her womb, she knew it was already too late. Making a quick mental note to call her GP first thing in the morning, she then felt a sudden, kinky thrill as she realised, for the third time in less than an hour, a man had climaxed inside her- and she liked it.

Good, I really have become a slut.

The thought sent a shudder of desire thundering through her body and the way her muscles tightened and convulsed around his cock, coupled with the feeling of Eric repeatedly hammering his prostate, pushed Victor over the edge. Shaking, his back curled and his shaven head fell back against the smaller male's shoulder. He exhaled a strangled squeak and drove into her arse to the hilt, his cock twitching, firing a thick tide deep into her brutalised bowels at the exact moment Eric succumbed to his own bliss and filled the burly giant's tight arse with cum.

Her muscles tensed, hungrily milking the shafts buried inside her, and Mina could tell her legs were on the verge of giving way as the hot fluids slashed against her inner walls, dicks pulsing. Nonetheless, by the way he throbbed against her tongue, and the increasingly desperate speed with which he was fucking her mouth, she could tell Charlie wasn't far behind his companions. With her vocalisations still reverberating down his length, the beauty, determined to finish him quickly, breathed in a deep breath through her nostrils then exhaled, sending a rush of warm air spilling across the organ, tickling the tip and caressing the sensitised glans.

"Ar-oh!" gasped Charlie in a choked splutter as, surprised and overwhelmed, he gave one last wild thrust all the way into her muggy orifice. His fingers tightened to a white-knuckled grip on the roots of her hair, forcing her to hold him in as his cock swelled and pulsed, shooting thick streams of salty cum down her throat. The sudden jet made Mina cough and splutter but, recovering quickly, she swallowed and drank down every drop, moaning happily, until his orgasm subsided.

And with that, the deed was done and Mina Carring, budding actress and glamour model, had experienced her first gangbang.

Seven

 Overwhelmed by the sheer force of the three simultaneous blasts, the foursome collapsed together in a huddle of sweaty bodies and tangled limbs. Panting hard as the afterglows burned through them, it was a full two minutes before any of them could muster the will to move, and then it was only to shakily stagger to their feet, withdrawing their softening shafts from her body and leaving the beauty huddled in a ball on the bedroom floor.

"Wo-wow... that... that was bloody brilliant..." panted Sean, his chest heaving and face suddenly as red as the hair covering his body, as he stumbled almost drunkenly about trying to pull his trousers over his legs. His companions each made similar remarks and comments of agreement, yet Mina was in no state to take note and only half watched them out of the corner of one eye while hugging her knees to her chin, trying to ignore the dull fire burning down between her thighs.

"Grr... there! You've got what you wanted!" Mark growled angrily, the low and deadly tone of his voice causing Mina to twist dazedly around to discover her stepbrother seething on his bed, his naked body almost shaking with inexpressible anger as he clutched the rumpled sheets with a bone-white grip. Beside him, Daniel sat poised, thin lips drawn tight and his handsome face overshadowed by a stern, emotionless mask, concealing his emotions. His muscles were tensed, a low tremor only just visible as it ran through him. He was prepared to spring at the slightest provocation. "Now destroy those fucking videos!"

Pulling his last article of clothing over his head, Sean appeared unmoved by the veiled threat and smirked broadly before reaching into his jean pocket and retrieved his phone. Unlocking the screen, he flicked through a few options before his eyes suddenly widened in a look of mock surprise that sent a surge of dread rushing down to the pit of Mina's stomach.

"Oh, I'm so sorry, we deleted those recordings ages ago. While you were watching Danny there fucking your sister, as it happens." His grin broadened and he turned the smartphone around to show them its empty gallery. "Didn't I mention it? Well, no harm done." He shrugged his shoulders offhandedly before turning his eyes down towards Mina, the cruel amusement reflected back at her making his irises gleam like quicksilver. "And after watching how wantonly she begged for both your cocks, we knew a slut like her wouldn't refuse us... if given the right incentive."

His words cut so deeply, Mina suddenly felt as if she'd been pitched through a sheet of thick ice and was plunging through the black frigid waters of a bottomless sea of self-loathing, the weight of her own disgust crushing down on her.

"You bastards!" Mark roared, but before either he or Daniel could rise, the group retreated, throwing open the bedroom door and slipping out in an instant, flooding the room with the sounds from the party still raging below, the inhabitants somehow gleefully oblivious to the activities having taken place above their heads. And as the door closed in her abusers' wake, muffling the uproar once more, Mina had never felt so desolate, so hopeless, so... lost.

Am I a slut?

The question rang hollow in her ears, a mocking whisper, taunting her as, in the back of her consciousness, she became aware of a warm, thick substance leaking from her pussy and rolling down her thighs.

Am I a slut?

She was not innocent, nor delusional enough to try to think of herself as one. She enjoyed sex. Even in her early teens, she had considered herself a sexual creature and had taken every opportunity to explore her sexuality. Yet never had she experienced anything like she had tonight, nor endured such a barrage of conflicting, thrilling sensations.

Am I a fucking slut?

She could say she'd had no choice, that she was doing it to save her career, or that it had been the only way she could protect Mark and save her family. Yet she could not lie to herself, and deep down she'd known, and she'd always know, that she'd liked it. She'd wanted it all. Everything, from the moment she'd stepped into the room to catch her stepbrother masturbating, and even getting gangbanged had played to her darker fantasies.

It was all so strange, so dirty. Although the merest thought of Sean and his cronies pawing at her body like ravenous hyenas devouring a baby antelope alive, made her skin crawl. The feeling of holding them all inside her, of being stretched and brutalised and dominated completely, was all at once so intense and yet woefully inadequate she had been brought to the brink of insanity. Even now, when the storm had passed, she could still feel the itch buzzing in her core, the liquid heat pulsing between her thighs, and she longed to suffer that maddening intensity once more, if only their clumsy stabbing had begun and released that slow burning ember deep inside her...

The soft, rhythmic thumping of feet walking across the floor broke her thoughts. Twisting towards the source of the commotion, the reverberations travelled through the carpet to echo in her ears, and she was slightly taken aback to discover Daniel and Mark standing over her, one broad and gloriously muscular, the other lean and spindly, both naked and hard as steel.

Oh, my God!

Eight

Her heart hammered excitedly as butter-flies fluttered in her stomach, and she opened her suddenly dry mouth to question them. Before she could utter a word, Daniel bent down, hooked both of his strong hands beneath her armpits and hoisted her up off the floor. Squealing in alarm, she instinctively threw her arms around his neck and held on for dear life as Danny crushed her to his muscular torso and trailed his hands down to grip her firm buttocks. Tipping her head back, she felt a hot thrill surge down her back at the look of hunger burning in his gaze an instant before his lips claimed her mouth in a demanding kiss of equal, raging passion.

Sensing his rampant arousal pressing against her swollen folds demanding entry, she could only moan into their embrace, teeth gnashing and tongues dancing, as he lowered her onto his shaft, a deep, lustful moan spilling from her lips at the feeling of the swollen crown splitting her folds and filling her depths. Still wet with desire, her body remembered his size and adjusted to his presence as she enveloped his hard cock inch by inch until he was fully sheathed within her snug embrace. Yet he did not linger and no sooner had he fully lowered her onto his shaft, he resumed fucking her, withdrawing almost all the way out before driving back in with a sudden upwards surge, raising a hard pounding rhythm, his hips rising and falling in hard, fast strokes while powerful hands supported her weight with ease.

Her back curled at the feeling of him passing in and out of her slit, driving into her over and over again with hard thrusts. The beauty tore her lips from his and tossed her head back, eyes bulging and mouth open, hollering a ragged cry at the repeated feeling of fullness reaching deep inside her, stretching her to capacity. Wrapping her long legs around his waist and crossing them over his tight, gyrating buttocks, pushing him even deeper into her warmth, she used the hold as leverage to rock upon his thick shaft as her core erupted with a fiery pleasure that emanated to the tips of her fingers and toes.

Sensing the fire-wreathed pressure gathering in her abdomen, marking the resurrection of her building climax rising like a phoenix from the ashes, Mina was certain no other lover had ever penetrated- no- had ever fucked her so deeply as this Adonis. Moving with him and meeting her lover plunge for maddening plunge, Mina could only moan and pant and scream with wild abandon. Carried by sheer burning desire, she rode him with all the feverish bravo of a cowgirl breaking a wild stallion and hungrily rammed herself down onto his hard shaft, her inner walls coaxed into grasping convulsions around the hard length every time he was fully embedded within her. "Oh wow- fuck... oh... yes... yes... fuck me! Fuck me!"

"Fuck... ugh, God! Your cunt's so small... so wet... yeah ride my dick, baby!" Grunting at the feeling of her innermost recesses tightening around his hard flesh, his nails bit into her succulent rump. Daniel heaved her up, raising her almost all the way off his shaft only to bring her crashing down as he thrust upward. They both shuddered and gasped ragged breaths as he forced her to take him deeper.

Delighting in the sudden shock of him splitting her open, Mina lost all self-control. Leaning back, her arms drawing tight and spine bowing, supported only by his powerful hands, she surrendered to his will as he began to drive into her with fresh vigour, this new angle giving him the perfect leverage with which to fuck her. Greedily consuming her offering like some great lustful beast of ancient mythos, Daniel brought her up and down in a fierce crashing tide of raw hunger and desire, his hips rocking and grinding against her pelvis with such intensity, as though intending to ruin her for any other lover to come after.

"Oh... oh... oh God! Your cock is so big... so deep... oh I can barely take it... Oh- fuck! Fuck! Fuck... so huge...incredible! Ah ...Yes... yes... YES!" His cock felt like a solid rod of titanium tightly wrapped in living silk, and was ripping her in half, reaching deep inside her, so very deep inside her he could barely fit. She was so wet, her nectar was rolling down her thighs in rivulets as his huge shaft moved in and out of her with ease, eliciting a wet, echoing, slapping resonance, and he was able to put himself as deep inside her as her body could take him and it felt so incredible. Eyes wide and mouth frozen agape, nearly screaming with each Herculean thrust, she could barely breathe through the inferno that overwhelmed her senses, pulsing through her veins with each quickening heartbeat as he sent her rushing towards her peak.

Seeming to sense that she was drawing close, he kept up his assault unchecked, fucking her in perfect time as he hoisted her up and down, his hard, steady strokes unaffected either by fatigue or by the pressure surely gathering in his loins, mounting bit by bit with each demonic thrust, building towards his inevitable creamy completion.

"Oh my God... Oh my God... It's too big... all the way- oh- in my stomach... but- omigod- so good... like you're splitting me in two... so good. Oh God, don't stop! Don't stop! Harder... fuck me harder... bounce me up and down on your dick... make me take it... give my tight pussy every fucking inch of your big oh- oh- oh!" Caught in the throes of ecstasy, she clawed his back, her perky breasts bounced with his rhythm, and his hands lifted and lowered her, controlling her like Sean and his henchmen had, as though she were nothing but a rag doll, but this was better.

The *la petite mort* almost upon her, she gazed up at him in utter rapture, held captive by the darkening storm of lust glazing his in fierce blue eyes, the intensity of his gaze drawing her into the very depths of his soul and she greedily sought to etch every part of his expression into her memory. The way his jaw tensed every time their bodies joined. It was the most erotic sight she had ever seen and proved to be just the catalyst she needed to finally push her over the edge. "Oh my God... oh... this is sooo... fucking good... oh shit! You're going to make me cum again... ah- ah- ah- ah- yes- yes- yes... you're going to make me cum... oh fuck yes! You're going to- omigod- omigod- I'm cumming, I'm cumming!"

It took all of a few moments, from start to summit, for him to bring her to climax. The dam broke. A pulse ripped through her body. Fiery pleasure blossomed in her abdomen, coursing through her veins in white-hot rivers of wildfire as she began to tremble uncontrollably, tossing her head from side to side, fireworks bursting behind both eyes, and lips spreading in a wide, toothy smile as the full force of the powerful orgasm washed over her.

In her delirium, she didn't notice Daniel's sideways glance, his subtle nod, or the shadowy form moving behind her as he continued pounding her. He hammered her relentlessly through the release, heightening her pleasure, sending her spiralling towards another even as her walls clamped down upon his throbbing shaft, holding him tight with all her might, and smothering him with her sticky nectar.

God, his stamina is amazi- Ow! What the fuck?

Seizing the moment, Mark had come upon her from behind. Taking advantage of his stepsister's distraction, he moved without making a sound, his long, dexterous fingers hooking over her hips to steady her as he manoeuvred into position. Lost in a fog of pleasure, her senses dulled by the powerful orgasm still raging through her, Mina sensed rather than felt the presence at her back and the swollen shaft rising between her already partially spread buttocks.

Mina's eyes widened, her limbs shaking all the more violently as her climax refused to subside, only seemed to grow all the stronger at the realisation of what was about to happen. The model and actress threw her head around but could only glimpse Mark out of the corner of her eye so looked up to find Daniel looking back at her knowingly. With a mischievous grin playing at the corner of his thin lips, he plunged into her warmth, her head spinning at the feeling of him stretching and filling her sensitised sheath, before tightening his grip on her to still her gyrating hips, holding her tightly against him as the head of her stepbrother's cock began to press against her anus.

After being broken-in by the stoic, squeaky Victor, her sphincter did not resist. Through the fog of fire and pulsing bliss, she felt an awesome pressure of hot, rubbery flesh forcing its way through the tight gateway of her flawless arse, popping easily past the ring of muscle and pressing her into Daniel. It hurt, but not as before. There was no pain, no burning agony, only a momentary numbness followed by an uncomfortable strained tightness, like she was already being stretched to her limit with only the head inside her. However, Mark was not done and continued to push his advantage, gently rocking back and forth on the balls of his feet, working centimetre after centimetre of his cock deep into the tight grip of her seamen-slickened bowels.

Whimpering softly, barely able to breathe through the intensity of the long length slowly filling her, goosebumps erupted all over her body and Mina curled forward to bite down, hard, upon Daniel's shoulder, tasting a splash of copper against the salt of his skin as her inner walls clenched involuntarily around him. His jaw tight, chiselled muscles bulging with the strain of remaining still, he groaned as her teeth grated painfully on bone while her plush sheath convulsed in vice-like contractions around his hard shaft. Then finally, with one last push, Mark had completely buried his whole cock in her luscious derrière and the turbulent concoction of pleasure mixing with the feeling of sheer, unparalleled fullness brought her to orgasm, right in the midst of her last.

They remained like that for a moment and in all her life, Mina had never felt so full. Pinned and suspended, sandwiched between her two young lovers, impaled upon their hard cocks, pressed fast against their hard bodies, their skin deliciously cool against the primal heat radiating from her core, it was as if every fibre of her being was stretched to accommodate these two studs. Visibly shaking as the force of the combined orgasms crashed over her, her pulse thundering in her ears and her vision dancing with white dots before her rolling eyes, she felt as if she were floating, and the last coherent part of her brain realised she was in real danger of losing consciousness. The embrace was so erotic however, that she couldn't have cared less and yearned for more as she began tingling from head to toe.

Two... two cocks feels so good!

"Oh -wow... fuck! Even after getting fucked by Victor, your asshole is still so tight, but don't worry Mina. I'll take care of that," she heard Mark promise through the haze that fogged her thoughts, just as her orgasms began to ebb. He sounded far away, yet his mouth was so close to her ear that she could feel his breath on the back of her neck, and she recognised that sinful, mischievous tone she knew all too well.

Then, without further ado, she felt him draw back, causing her entire body to shudder as her arse tensed, sucking at his shaft and trying to hold him in. He carried on regardless, his motions slow and purposeful, gradually dragging half his length from her bowel's embrace before pushing back in a little more firmly, then repeating the process, siring a rhythm that quickly had her eyes squeezed shut from sensory overload.

Clinging to Daniel as if her life depended upon it, as though he were her very anchor to reality, a pained whimper escaped Mina, the slight sting of her muscles stretching to accommodate so much pressure, until her arse began to relax, giving way to such a deep sense of pleasure. No doubt able to feel her body opening up to him, Mark held nothing back, withdrawing until only the bulbous crown remained inside her tight bowels and then slamming back in, making his stepsister's eyes pop open in surprise.

"Ah! Oh- yes!" she moaned into Daniel's shoulder, her heart pounding and nails biting deep half-moons into the hard muscles of his back as she felt the solid heat of Mark's dick sawing in and out of her arse. The sensation was so intense and wildly exciting that she thought she would combust, and she could feel her body shake, the pounding pressure, coupled with her awesome feeling of fullness and the huge cock that pulsed and throbbed deep within her, flooding her consciousness with the rawest sense of pleasure.

Yet before she could begin to comprehend the physicality of her lust, Daniel broke his fast and resumed rolling his hips, churning and grinding into her warmth, and the feeling of them both suddenly moving inside her had her throw her head back, a voiceless cry billowing from her rosy lips as every nerve in her clitoris went supernova.

Working together, the pair forged a relentless rhythm with one driving in while the other withdrew, thrusting-drawing- thrusting- drawing...

"Oh- my- God, oh- my- God, oh- my- holy... fuck!" Eyes wide and mewing breathlessly, Mina felt like she was about to combust from the delicious friction of both cocks moving inside her, rubbing against the thin membrane that divided them, making her pussy run wet with dew.

It was torture. It was ecstasy, as absolute as it was un-bearable. Losing herself in the feeling of being so full, so stretched, of arms encompassing her and hot flesh rubbing against her skin, Mina constantly needed to remind herself to breathe as her sense of awareness leapt between the huge cock stretching her sex, the deep sense of fullness radiating through her arse and the needy throbbing of her clit. Overwhelmed, her body began to add its own motions, twisting, wriggling, and riding the hard shafts, her muscles convulsing as the inner walls of her pussy and rectum grew swollen and oversensitive, dissolving into writhing spirals.

"Fuck... your pussy's getting tighter," Danny growled, the deep resonance of his voice sending hot shivers down her spine. It was then she noticed his handsome face tilted towards her, his jaw tight and those piercing blue eyes dark with lust, watching her with a smouldering intensity that had her stomach winding into tight knots. "And that expression is so sexy. Do you really love taking two cocks at once so much?" He was emphasising each word with a hard thrust, his pelvic bone teasing her clit. "Why don't you tell us which you like best, Mina? What's better, my dick in your pussy or your brother's in that tight little asshole?"

"Urgh... I ca-can't decide... they both feel so good! Oh Fuck- oh fuck- oh fuck... I'm so- so full- oh fuck- fuck!" Deep down, she knew the question should have repulsed her, yet his words were so coarse and dirty, it only excited her further. "Oh, boys... oh, boys... oh- oh you're such bad, dirty boys... oh- my- God... I love it... fuck me harder... yes... yes..."

She was a vision of passion, rocking and bouncing and grinding between them, perky breasts jiggling, her features contorted with unearthly pleasure, and urging them on amidst ragged breaths. Her orgasm built like a great black storm upon the horizon.

This wasn't like it had been with Sean and his little friends. That had been so different, so violent and primitive, with them using her as a piece of meat, a tool for their own gratification. None of it could have prepared her for this, carnal instinct coursing through her veins. The intensity, the friction, the fullness, the sheer... feeling of it all, nothing was as it should be. She was just so sensitive, every feeling felt amplified and enhanced, pushing her towards the highest pinnacle of pleasure as heat- glorious, orgasmic fire- reached out from her core, spreading through every fibre of her being to consume her. Body and soul. Goddamn, it was too good.

"Oh fuck, Mina... your ass is amazing!" Mark groaned into her ear. His breath washed over the back of her neck and sent hot shivers down her spine. "It's so tight and slippery and- fuck- squeezing my dick so tightly... ugh... God, this is the greatest birthday present ever!"

Somewhere in the dark forgotten recesses of her brain, Mina registered Danny growling something in response, but she couldn't make sense of his words through the sudden fog of pleasure blanketing her thoughts. A sparkle caught her eye, a twinkle of starlight falling though the heavens. Peering through the haze, she discerned a bead of sweat trickling down his neck, leaving a glistening trail down his stretched skin. Entranced, she leant forward to scoop up the bead of perspiration before dragging her tongue back up his slick skin, delighting in the salty flavour. A low growl emanated from Daniel, before she took the lobe of his ear between her teeth. She suckled it wantonly, her every thought focused on teasing the fleshy nub until an anonymous hand suddenly slapped her stretched backside and the shock of the sting had her release the lobe in a surprised gasp, her head rolling back onto Mark's shoulder. Not missing a beat, her step-brother claimed her mouth in a hungry kiss, his silky tongue sweeping past her bruised and swollen lips to pillage hers, while another set of lips suddenly enveloped her right breast, sucking greedily and sending electricity zipping through her bosom.

Relishing their touch, her back curled, arching into Daniel's mouth as his tongue circled her pebbled nipple, offering herself to him while slipping one of her hands from his shoulder and dragging her manicured nails down his broad torso before coiling the limb back around Mark's neck. Drunk on the hot, tingling sensations that were coursing through her body, she kissed him back with equal hunger, teeth gnashing and tongues duelling, nearly devouring him with her need. Her senses were ablaze and her whole world suddenly shrank down to just the feeling of the fierce fires raging in her core, the silky tongue circling and lashing her oversensitive bud, and the shafts sliding back and forth, impaling her, pounding her, fucking her. Oh, God, she was so close, she felt like she was about to burst. This wasn't sex. She was sex. *She* was sex embodied and personified, from the molten fires raging in her core to the desperate need pulsing through her clit and the tingling in her fingertips. She was Aphrodite. She was Isis. She was Venus. She was the goddess and the moon and the stars above.

Yes! I'm a slut, and God save me, I love it! I fucking love it! I-I...

"Urgh..." Mina gasped, dragging her mouth from Mark's, before she threw her head back and a desperate, primitive sound burst from her lips as the sudden epiphany sent the tight knot of fiery tension at her centre supernova.

In that moment, time seemed to hold its breath and she had a sudden inexplicable sense of rising before the calm abruptly descended upon her. Frozen in a state of limbo, with all perceptions of time forgotten, her heartbeat roaring in her ears and her body vibrating with a subtle, inexpressible tension, she hung upon that precipice for what seemed an eternity before finally plummeting back down to earth, her climax surging over her with raging intensity. Eyes rolling, muscles clenching, she desperately tried to give voice to her pleasure, but the words stuck in her throat and all that escaped was a strangled gasp before she began to tremble and writhe uncontrollably in her lovers' arms, the waves of pleasure ripping through her, sweeping her away on a tide of euphoria.

Daniel and Mark weren't done with her, however, and beneath the storm of fire and ecstasy Mina could feel them quickening inside her, their synchronised rhythm coming undone as her inner walls convulsed around them, becoming rougher, wilder and more erratic, then falling apart completely.

Mark was the first to break.

"Oh fuck, Mina, It's so hot watching you cu- fuck- fuck..." he grunted, the moist warmth of his breath spilling over the sensitive spot that joined her neck and shoulder in short, quick gasps. His mouth attacked the side of her neck, the wetness of his tongue swirling over her sweet spots in a way he knew drove her wild. He was close, the rational, almost dormant part of her mind warned, and true to her prediction, moments later his thrusts began hastening with the urgency of his nearing release.

Her stepbrother held nothing back, driving into her with a quick, furious tempo that made her arse feel electrified and had her rebounding against Daniel's motions in the perfect angle for his pelvis to continue rubbing against her throbbing clit, the repeating friction causing sunspots to flicker before her eyes.

Yet Daniel only groaned at the feeling of her muscles clenching around him, the low sound reverberating through her bosom while his tongue flittered over her painfully stiff nipple. His strokes were growing ever more intense and purposeful, making her feel every inch, ridge and, vein of the magnificent cock ramming into her, the mushroom-shaped head striking her deepest, sweetest spots with each plunge, birthing writhing tongues of white fire that surged through her pulsing core to the tips of her fingers and toes.

They were relentless, never slowing, their powerful hands squeezing the firm mounds of her arse with bruising intensity, supporting her and manipulating her, fucking her, pushing her on, dragging her orgasm out longer and longer and making her tingle from head to toe. They moved as one but at the same time with complete indifference to each other, together but also separate, one fucking her with wild abandon, the other playing her body with all the precision and skill of a London orchestra. Losing all control, she could do nought but cling to them for dear life, utterly at their mercy, their low moans filling her ears and the musky aroma of sex infesting every breath. The waves grew and lengthened, sweeping over her with greater and greater force until she could no longer tell where one ended and the next began.

"...Fucking dicks... oh yeah... give them to me... yes... yes-yes- ah- ah- ah!" The words burst from her in a ragged cry as she tried to snatch life-preserving breaths amidst a crescendo of sobbing cries, the world spinning around their tangled bodies. Even before the waves had passed, her body was mounting the crest of another climax, the fires sweeping through her... No, she had to stop, needed to catch her breath, she couldn't take it, it was too good, too...

Hot. I'm so... so hot... my pussy... my ass... they're melting... Oh God... no! It's too much... I'm going crazy... I'm going... I'm going...

Unable to stay in sync, they rammed into her with unbridled vigour, their hips slapping wetly against her skin as her nectar ran down her thighs in rivulets, each powerful thrust driving her against the next, so deep she could almost feel their cocks meeting in her stomach. Then, seemingly by chance, they both slammed into her at once and that sudden sweet shock of incredible fullness cast her spirit from her body, from the mass of tangled flesh, through the roof, into the night sky above, soaring through the heavens until, finally, darkness enveloped her.

Nine

Somewhere a phone was ringing.

It sounded far away, yet too near for her to ignore, like a subtle voice in the wind, whispering to her through the thick morning fog and dragging her from the warm cocoon that enveloped her.

Half asleep and reluctant to lose the welcoming comfort of sleep's embrace, she rolled over and buried her face in her pillow, stubbornly trying to block out the interruption before groaning a low, mournful sound, surrendering to the inevitable. With her eyes still shut and the phone's shrill ringing echoing in her ears, though sounding distinctly closer now, she sat up, causing the duvet covering her to cascade down her front, revealing her creamy skin and pert breasts.

Stretching her arms out above her head, her muscles stiff from her long slumber, she then rubbed the sleep from her eyes with the base of her palm before opening them enough to discern the first grey light of dawn filtering into the room, shrouding it in gloom. Blurry-eyed, she had to blink thrice before the world slipped into focus.

Mina didn't remember falling asleep. She felt exhausted, drained, and so very weary. Her eyes were heavy and her throat parched with a salty, bitter flavour souring the back of her mouth. Oddly, there was also a dull, but oddly satisfying soreness throbbing in her lower abdomen. What recollections she had were like the memories of a dream she had just awoken from but already forgotten, a dream of tangled, naked bodies writhing in passion.

She'd expected to awake in her bright cavernous bedroom, snuggled in her goose feather bed and luxurious Egyptian cotton duvet, but the weak morning light revealed a small cluttered chamber with poster-adorned pale grey-blue walls. The air was heavy with a stale musky odour and wherever she looked there was rumpled clothing scattered across the dark charcoal carpet.

Mark's bedroom!

Icy realisation dawned. Throwing off the sheets and scrambling out of bed, she bolted across the room, her long legs wobbling dangerously with every step, before diving for her jacket amidst the scattered garments. Fishing through the pockets, taunted by the repeating buzz of the vibrate alarm, she finally managed to withdraw the phone only to catch a momentary glimpse of Jason's photo on the caller ID before it died in her hand.

Cursing under her breath, she activated the screen. Sure enough, there were at least half a dozen missed calls from Jason, as well as twice that many texts and two, no doubt very scathing, audio messages. Releasing a heavy breath she hadn't realised she'd been holding, Mina had a sudden overwhelming urge to hurl the device to the floor and stomp on it.

Like all directors, Jason tended to overreact, though in this case she supposed his suspicions would not be entirely unjustified. No doubt there would be some very tricky questions to answer when she got home. And if the number of missed calls was any indication, it was going to take all of her skills to smooth this one over, and she certainly meant *all* of them.

Her head snapped up at the sound of rustling, eyes darting towards the source of the disturbance. Mark was asleep on the bed, rolling onto his side with one hand buried beneath a pillow while the other dragged a handful of the bedsheets to his chest, his narrow, boyishly handsome face covered by a stray wing of wispy, chocolate-coloured hair.

There was no sign of Daniel, though in the cold light of day, or rather early morning, she supposed that was probably a very good thing. In her current mood, she wasn't sure if she would have killed him, or pounced and taken him for another five rounds. The sight of him had a smile tugging at the corner of her lips. She loved Jason and she would miss him. They had had many good times together and the thought of losing him left a sickly feeling in the bottom of her gut. Yet if the day ever came when she had to choose, there would only ever be one winner. Yet that was by no means the sum of her troubles.

Daniel. Sean. Charlie. Eric. Victor. She had bought their silence and complacency with her body, and they had deleted their recordings as agreed. However, nothing could undo what they had seen. Mina's stomach tightened at the thought. Maybe, if she was inexplicably lucky, all four would hold their tongues, taking the secret to their graves, but that was a gamble of long odds. It would only take one slip to let the cat out of the bag.

No, she knew it was inevitable, whether slurred amidst a drunken rant or as an anonymous tip given pride of place on the cover of some gossiping celebrity trash magazine, the truth would come out. It was only a matter of time.

Her innards churned with a sudden sense of hopelessness, but Mina tried to put it to the back of her mind. She wished she knew what to do. There was nothing she wouldn't give, nothing she wouldn't do, to protect Mark. He was more than her stepbrother, more than a lover. He completed her, made her feel whole in a way no one else ever had, or could, and for him she knew she'd relive last night all over again without a moment's hesitation. However, when that awful day of reckoning arrived, could she protect him?

Tears began to burn the corners of her eyes. Quickly blinking the unshed moisture away, she cast a rueful look back at Mark, watching him sleep until a reluctant smile tugged at the corner of her lips. A storm was coming, but no matter what devastation it would unleash upon them, they would face it together, as they always did.

Grabbing what comfort she could from that thought, Mina quickly turned off the phone and slipped it back into her jacket. She would need it later, when she made that grovelling call to Jason, apologising for not coming home, insisting she'd merely lost track of time and spent the night kipping on her father's bed. But for now, all she wanted to do was have a shower.

Clambering awkwardly to her feet, she gathered up her clothes from the floor and folded and placed them neatly in a pile at the foot of the bed before tiptoeing across the room. Lingering by the door, she took one final look back, smiling fondly as she etched the image of Mark sleeping into her memory. Turning back, she grasped the handle, eased the door open a crack and slipped silently through, pulling it closed as she went without making a sound.

The hallway was inky black. Pressing her back against the door, the wood cool against her skin, Mina waited with bated breath, her ears peeled for the slightest sound, yet the house was as still and silent as the grave. When she was certain she was alone, she let the breath go in a heavy sigh. Turning on her heel, she hurried past the closed door of her father's empty room and past the framed family pictures she knew were hanging upon the walls, masked by darkness, their unseeing eyes watching her naked body pass with voyeur's delight. Her feet padded with every step, the carpet soft underfoot, and she moved quickly, silently, and with all the grace and elegance of a stalking tigress towards the far door, pausing only when she came to the mouth of the stairs.

Hugging the wall, she edged forward and peered around the bend, but the foyer below was vacant except for the crumpled Styrofoam cups, crisp packets, a pizza box, and a mass of other rubbish littering the faded carpet.

Damn punks, Dad will freak if he sees this mess!

Still reluctant to pass through the shafts of light blazing from the floor below for fear of being spotted by some hungover reveller just waking from a drunken slumber and stumbling into the foyer, she drew back. Taking a breath, gathering her courage, she raised her leg, and then the deed was done.

With the sun warm upon her skin, she sprang the gap into the cloak of darkness and ran the last few steps to the bathroom. Throwing open the door, she darted in without a backwards glance.

Long and narrow, with deep blue walls and white vinyl floor tiles, the bathroom was the smallest room in the house. With a tug of the pull switch, the thin chamber flooded with bright yellow luminescence that belied the weak light trickling through the frosted glass of the only window. Noting the already drawn shower curtain around the bath, she reached in, turned the shower temperature dial to full, pushed the power button and quickly withdrew the arm just before she heard the rush of water and the pitter-patter against the cloth. Whilst waiting for the water temperature to rise, she busied herself with taking a neatly folded towel from one of the shelves of the tall linen cabinet and hung it on the towel rail, taking care as she did not to glance at the mirror above the sink. She would not dare to look at her reflection, fearful of who, or what, she'd see staring back at her.

Pulling back the curtain, releasing a great billowing plume of steam, Mina clambered into the bath and stepped under the spray. Letting out a contented sigh as the scalding water cascaded down her naked body, slowly turning her creamy skin baby pink, she stood motionless beneath the pelting torrent with her head tipped back, letting it purge her, cleanse her and wash away all remnants of the night before and then carry her away. Completely engrossed in the shower, she didn't notice the dull creak of the bathroom door opening and closing.

A warm fog enveloped her. The heat was therapeutic and reached deep inside her, soothing the dull ache in her abdomen, the proof that last night had been anything but a dream. Feeling the stress flow from her body, she took a bottle of citrus-fresh shower gel from the caddy hanging off the fixtures, popped the cap and squeezed a generous portion of the lemon-scented substance onto her palm. Closing and replacing the bottle back on the shelf, she began washing her arms, purring with delight as she did at the silky sensuality of her hands moving across her skin, her heart suddenly pounding beneath her breast.

There was something so... sexual, about washing in the shower. Surrendering to impulse and letting her hands work their magic, they slid down her flanks, down her smooth thighs and drew perilously close to the folds of her womanhood before rising, gliding ever so lightly up the flat plane of her belly to cup her breasts, her nipples rising beneath her soapy palms. Her heart beating fast, she bit back a moan as she began to roll the pebbled buds between her thumbs and forefingers, sending a tingle surging down to her centre.

I am a slut.

There was a sudden damp rustle, and a frigid breeze brushed her skin. Her head whipped around to discover Mark standing over her. He was completely naked and an almost inaudible groan escaped her as she watched him step over the rim of the tub, her greedy eyes drinking in his tight buttocks and bobbing erection, before realising how she must have looked. She dropped her hands to her sides, her cheeks burning with a sudden nervous blush.

Mark pulled the curtain closed behind him with a gentle tug before turning to confront her, his eyes gleaming with dark, predatory hunger, the spray plastering his fringe to his forehead. She could feel his gaze upon her soapy breasts. Feeling suddenly embarrassed, she tried to say something but before she could fathom a word, he closed the gap between them and claimed her mouth in a deep, devouring kiss, his arms coiling about her waist and pulling her against him, his engorged arousal poking against her hip.

Here we go again.

The End

If you enjoyed Uncovered, why not try one of these steamy dark romances

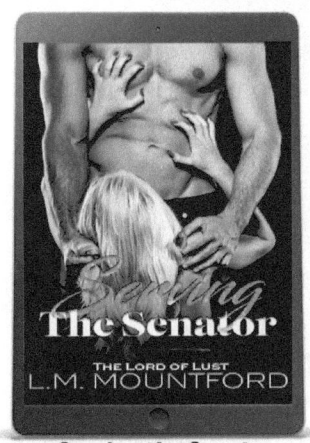 

Serving the Senator **Rogue**

Learn more at LMMountford.com

Washington State was beautiful in Autumn.

The weather was fucking awful, but it was still beautiful.

Beneath the thick canopy of grey storm clouds, the forests of the Olympic Peninsula's northern slopes were a riot of colour. A wondrous collage of yellows, reds and oranges, amidst a sea of lush green that was all the more vivid amidst the gloom of an impending downpour. In the morning, the air was alive with birdsong, while the evenings rang to the haunting chorus of the Roosevelt Elk that grazed across the land.

Unfortunately, now there was only the roar of the Chevrolet Suburban's engine as it navigated up the winding dirt road.

I watched it come from the rocking chair on my balcony, hoping they were just some thick-as-shit ramblers that had got themselves lost on the Clallam Bay Trail, but I wasn't that hopeful. The trail started a good 10 miles down the

Strait of Juan de Fuca Highway, in the so-named town, and never left the highway.

Even Ray Charles couldn't miss the signs.

Then again, I didn't have visitors.

You don't go through the hassle of leasing land on the Makah reservation if you want a roaring social life.

The Tribal Council's price was extortionate, but it was worth it. No visitors. No nosy neighbours. Not even the odd Jehovah's Witness trying his luck with the *'heathens'*.

The community and I had an understanding. If I left them alone, they'd leave me alone. Apart from my occasional trip up to Neah Bay for supplies, they had practically no idea I even existed. Which worked just fine for me.

Which begged the question, whose SUV was that driving up my driveway?

Well, there was only one way to find out. Maybe they were just going to ask for directions. They clearly couldn't read. I'd put up Private property signs everywhere.

I met them at the door just as the Grey Suburban pulled up. The passenger door opened, and King Kong, dressed in a poor fitting black suit and shades, stepped out. One look had my mind jumping to the Remington 870 12Gauge and the SIG 9mm in my weapons locker, just out of sight of the barn doors and just out of reach.

Then the Driver's door opened and this time Donkey Kong stepped out, done up in a matching costume. Maybe Ray-Ban had a two for one sale on. Then he stepped round to open the back door, and King Louie stepped down. Middle-aged and smaller, but dressed in a much nicer suit than his pair of gorillas, this guy was clearly the money.

No shades though, maybe Ray-Ban didn't have something to go with the Harris Tweed. Probably for the best. Sunglasses would suit that pudgy face and bald pate encircled by tufts of curly ginger hair about as well as tits on a bull.

"Mr Greystoke?"

He said my name without a stutter, but his voice trembled all the same beneath that smooth, business-like manner. He was nervous.

Good, he should be. I didn't like uninvited guests.

I ignored his question, and his minders, and looked him dead in the eye. "If you're lost, the highway is back that way, past the keep out signs."

His sallow face dropped, his business-like mask faltering slightly as he licked his lips, but he kept on. "Ah, no, no we're not lost, Mr Greystoke." He extended his hand, a bold gold signet ring dressing one chubby sausage finger. "My name is Ritter, Jiles Ritter, and I have some business to discuss with you."

I glared at him until the hand dropped back to his side. "Well, I don't want any, and I'm not buying."

"I'm not here to sell you anything, Mr Greystoke. I'm buying."

"Well, I'm not selling." Bored with conversation, I turned to head back inside. "Be sure to use a low gear when the track goes down the hill or your brakes will go."

Out of the corner of my eye, I glimpsed Donkey Kong stepping forward, no doubt having half a mind, in more than one sense, to stop me. I steeled myself to put the Gorilla down, knowing I'd need to do it fast, before King Kong could join in. But then Ritter got a word in first. "Mrs Bourne recommended you. Says you're just the sort of man I'm looking for."

I paused mid-step and threw a curious look back. "Elvira Bourne?" I waited for him to bite. It was easy to pick a name out of a glossy magazine full of the rich and famous. In my line, I could have worked for any of them.

He looked confused for a moment, as if trying to place the name, then embarrassedly corrected me. "Err... Elizabeth, and her ex-husband."

Ahhh... now it all made sense. Mrs Elizabeth Bourne, or rather Crane, as she now was. She'd needed my help a few months ago persuading her *philanthropist* husband, who was to music what Harvey Weinstein was to films, to give her a divorce. An easy enough task in itself, but not, however, when you considered the ironclad prenup, the young and then lovesick, soon to be Mrs Bourne had signed without a second thought. She'd needed a way around it.

The terms were simple enough. The then Mrs Elizabeth Bourne got nothing unless her husband did something stupid and got it splashed all over the tabloids. Scandal and humiliation were the cancer of the rich and famous. It had been my pleasure to facilitate it, with the help of two call girls with dreams of being photographers, a farmer, or rather a few of his barnyard pigs, and a healthy but non-threatening dose of drugs that would put Mr Bourne out like a light, and hard as a rock.

No doubt the newly single, and very grateful, Mis Crane had recommended me after hearing about whatever trouble this guy had got himself into.

"Come inside." I was about to lead him in, then paused, thought better of it, and glanced back over my shoulder. "Just you, the Gorillas stay outside."

I'd read somewhere that the land had once belonged to a horse rancher who'd bought it from the tribal council in 1922. Unfortunately, the market crash of 29 hit his interests hard and while drowning his sorrows, he managed to set fire to the main house while he was passed out inside it. In the years that followed, the ground remained unused until the Tribal council finally won their legal battle to have the land returned to them in 1994, when all traces of the main house's gutted structure were gone.

Somehow untouched in the fire, the barn had survived, more or less, and the council had converted the rafters into an open plan studio flat. The ground level remained much as it had back in the good old days, a large, open space, with a row of stalls along the back wall. My land cruiser sat in the one on the end, undercover and in dire need of servicing. Behind it, the diesel generator coughed and sputtered like a smoker on fifty-a-day in its cupboard.

I avoided the stairs leading to the flat and circled the old rustic desk with a frayed dark green leather topper that took up the centre of the space to sit in the chair. Ritter remained standing. There wasn't a second chair, and I didn't intend to offer him one. Outside, the gorillas waited by the car. I ignored them and fixed my gaze on the small man.

"Right," I barked. "So, first things fucking last, Mr Ritter, never come to my place unannounced again. You want to see me, you make an appointment like everyone else, got it?"

"Yes," he nodded, his head bobbing in a way that made him look a bit like a penguin.

Having established that one important fact, I relaxed back into my chair and steepled my fingers together. "So, what's this business?"

"Well, you see Mr Greystoke... err," he seemed torn between relief and nervousness. "I'm not quite sure how to say this, this isn't exactly the sort of thing I'm accustomed to."

Feeling the tale-tale throbbing of a headache starting, I resist the urge to massage my temples, already regretting the decision to hear him out. "Well, just start from the beginning, Mr Ritter, and see where that goes. You'll probably find it gets easier as you go on."

"Well, it's just that it's been months now, and they haven't paid me back, not a cent. I can't wait any longer."

"You owe money?" I ask, my interest peaked. This guy certainly didn't look the sort that shopped at Good Will and Oxfam. Unless they'd opened up a branch on Savile Row in the last month and the story hadn't broken yet.

He paled at the suggestion. "No, it's my partner. He's very displeased. It wasn't his money, you understand, but he says that outstanding debts owed to our consortium, even if it's only on paper, are bad for business. He thinks it makes him look weak, by association."

A partner?

The idea intrigued me.

Sounded like Mr Ritter had wanted to swim with the big boys but instead found himself in the shark tank and was just managing to hold his head above water.

"So why come to me? You've got lawyers. Let the courts handle this."

"That would take too long," he spluttered, sweat misting his forehead. "Please, Mr Greystoke. I need the money back by Friday evening, before the banks close."

I checked my watch. It was Monday, a little after nine in the morning. Not a lot of time then. Difficult, but not impossible. There was a clunk outside, and my eyes darted to the door. The minders must have got bored because they'd started fishing around inside the SUV. "Well, what about your two friends out there? They're big lads. They should be able to handle this for you."

"Oh No, Mark and Luke, no, no, no, that wouldn't do at all. I'm a well-known man, Mr Greystoke. I have friends, business associates, and they know their faces. If something went wrong and word got out, it would all come back to me. Any hint of violence or criminal activity would ruin me."

I resisted the impulse to ask which one was Luke and which was Mark. They looked pretty much identical to me. With their broad barrel builds and sloping temples, Donkey and King suited them much better.

"But you do want your money, right?" My headache was growing, and this time I couldn't help but rub my temples. Never mind minders, this guy needed a fucking nanny.

"I need it, Mr Greystoke, by Friday." And the look on his face was so desperate, I thought he might drop to one knee and start kissing my arse.

"Very well, just write down their names and addresses, the amounts they owe, and how long for." I pulled out a pad of writing paper and a pen from the desk draw, slapped them down on the topper and slid them over to him.

He did so, in a scribble so quick it was only just legible, then slid it back to me. "There, please, Mr Greystoke, I can't wait any longer."

I looked them over. Three names. All relatively local, not considerable sums, though the amount for number three meant he might be a problem. That one would definitely need some convincing, maybe a bit of arm twisting... or breaking.

Hopefully, it wouldn't go that far, but you never knew.

I looked Ritter in the eye, letting him know I was deadly serious. "I'll get you your money, Mr Ritter, don't worry, but this isn't a charity. My fee is fifteen percent, plus expenses, understand?"

"Of course, don't worry, you'll have it. Just hurry, please."

I nodded in understanding.

And with that, we were done. He turned and hurried out of the barn, back to the SUV.

I watched them drive away from my chair until the Suburban was out of sight. My phone vibrated in my pocket. Unlocking the screen with my fingerprint, it came alive to show a camera's live feed. It was motion-sensitive, one of several I'd rigged up all around the ground. The SUV moved into screen and two symbols appeared at the bottom, red circles with the legend *BOOM*.

My thumb hovered over one, and it sorely tempted me to blow Mr Rigger and the Kong brothers straight to hell for a moment. God, it would be so easy.

Instead, I closed the app and opened up the web browser.

Within a few clicks, I'd learned almost everything there was to know about Jiles Ritter. It was boring stuff.

Unmarried. No kids. A financier of various small-scale businesses and organisations, all legitimate. So, what sort of partner could he have that would make him so nervous?

Satisfied but curious, I put my phone on the table and went upstairs to get dressed into something more suitable.

I had work to do.

And what fun it would be.

No violence. I laughed out loud at that. Mr Ritter clearly lived in a comfy little padded cell, or just in Never Never Land. Just how did he expect me to get his money back in a few days without banging a few heads together? Yell trick-or-treat at them?

Money lending was a dirty business. When the debts went unpaid, that didn't leave many avenues for collection.

Outside, the rains began.

+++

Grab your copy today to continue reading John's adventure

Connect with other readers who enjoyed Uncovered in my **Facebook reader group** *or* **Join our newsletter** *for secret sneak peeks and exclusive bonuses.*
Lastly, don't forget to ***follow me wherever you hang out*** *for future updates, discounts, or behind the scenes looks!*

Also by the Author

From the insidious mind of The Lord of Lust, author L.M.
Mountford, comes an incredible omnibus of more than a
dozen books that'll keep you on the edge of your seat from
the first page to the last.

A Steamy Romance Boxset by The Lord of Lust

7 Books, 7 hard and rugged men, 7 sizzling page turners that will have you devouring every word from start to finish...

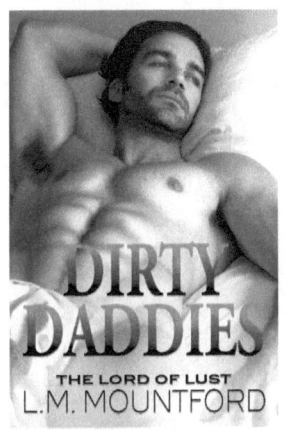

An Older Man Younger Woman Age Gap Romance Collection

The Politician. The Billionaire. The Detective. Three hot alpha males. Three steamy older men, younger woman age gap romances.

I know it's wrong to want my best friend's dad... but what about when his wife offers to share? Tracey has known the Burtons practically all her life. They're her best friend's parents. When she was a little girl they took her on days out to the beach. But she's a woman now, and they have some very important lessons to teach her...

About the Author

L.M. Mountford's goal in life is to be unique, a character who stands out from the crowd that you just can't help remembering with a bemused chuckle.

A born and bred country boy from the southwest of England, he knew from an early age that he wanted to write and spent most of his time writing story ideas or playing Star Wars on his PlayStation.

Not much has changed over the years, though his stories have grown decidedly dirtier, and he swapped the Star Wars for Call of Duty.

Dubbed the Lord of Lust in 2019 and a firm believer that nothing sells like sex and violence, he loves writing about hard and gritty romantic thrillers, loaded with action men, sassy heroines, and a whole lot of dirty, sexy heat.

He also loves meeting and chatting with readers who love his work. You can connect with him on facebook, or subscribe to his newsletter for regular updates.